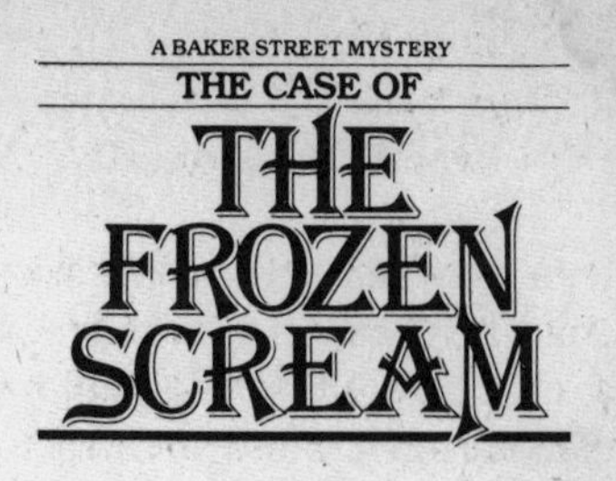
A BAKER STREET MYSTERY
THE CASE OF
THE
FROZEN
SCREAM

A BAKER STREET MYSTERY

THE CASE OF

THE FROZEN SCREAM

Thomas Brace Haughey

Bethany Fellowship INC.
MINNEAPOLIS, MINNESOTA 55438

The Case of the Frozen Scream
by Thomas Brace Haughey
Illustrations by Ken Lochhead

Library of Congress Catalog Card Number 79-50829

ISBN 0-87123-045-3

Published by Bethany Fellowship, Inc.
6820 Auto Club Road
Minneapolis, Minnesota 55438

Printed in the United States of America

Dedication

To Dr. Homero Rivas who scaled Mount Mc-Kinley, Julian Silva who rode the London underground, and my wife, Linda, who was snowed under with typing.

THOMAS BRACE HAUGHEY is the English Program Director of missionary radio station KVMV-FM in McAllen, Texas. He received his bachelor's degree from the University of Maryland, in 1965, and a Th.M. from Capital Bible Seminary in 1969. In addition, he received a diploma from Rio Grande Bible Institute Language School. While at the University of Maryland, he was inducted into the literary honorary society, Phi Delta Epsilon. He has done evangelism and youth work in Mexico, and taught for a year and a half in a missionary Bible school. His experience as a writer includes: Editing a Jesus Paper, writing numerous articles, writing scripts for "Folk Festival," a weekly radio program, and more than 100 book reviews each year for broadcast. His first book is *The Case of the Invisible Thief*, the first volume of the Baker Street Mystery series, Bethany Fellowship, Inc., 1978. Mr. Haughey is married, has one daughter, and makes his home in McAllen, Texas.

Preface

At the turn of the century the detective story was considered in the same light as the soap opera. It was an inferior form of literature written by and primarily read by men. How that has changed! Talented authors including such women as Agatha Christie and Dorothy Sayers have given literary respectability to the detective story. And the number of people reading and watching mysteries has enlarged to include almost everyone. A glance at current television ratings offers ample evidence of the trend. No less than seven of the fifty most popular programs are detective dramas—despite the substandard plots, poor dialogue, and cheap sensationalism that often characterize TV "who-done-its."

The best modern-day mysteries, however, well deserve the kudos they receive. Whether consciously or subconsciously, the public has recognized an extraordinary potential for good woven into the plots of these dramas. Surveys show that even those people most adamently opposed to media violence watch or read mysteries. Why? The answer isn't hard to find. The detective novel, as Dorothy Sayers has observed, is the most moral of all tales. It does not glorify the perverse but rather exposes it—endorsing the biblical principle that a person's sin will find him out. The sleuth is a representative of virtue. He battles against and ultimately subdues evil. He despises the cruelty and dishonesty that he encounters. And he defends the helpless. He is, in other words, a trench coat hero—almost a prophet in trench coat.

In light of the ethical nature of the job, it is remarkable to me that so few detectives have been evangelicals. Peter Wimsey, to be sure, met suspects who showed signs of piety. But he himself was not a Christian. The Sugar Creek gang, Lori Adams, and Jim Dunlap were all born again. But they were teenagers or younger. Where is the adult detective who does more than defend some meaningless status quo? Where is the man whose morality is based upon friendship with the God who stands above and ordains law? To my knowledge there are only two—Geoffrey Weston and his assistant John Taylor, Esq. And even Geoffrey was not a Christian when he first took up fingerprint powder and magnifier. The Inklings disbanded long before his admittance to Oxford, so he was never exposed to their stimulating theological debates. Nor were his years in the R.A.F. productive—except to confirm his dean's earlier suspicion that he was an inveterate dabbler. Weston didn't really find himself professionally until he set up shop at Number 31, Baker Street. And it was not until later, as a result of his investigation into the strange disappearance of Jessica Worthington's corpse (a story reserved for another volume), that he became a believer.

In this adventure Weston and Taylor almost lose their lives trying to solve the most chilling mystery of their career. A corpse is seen grading papers. A monkey doesn't play mumblety-peg. And our detectives look beyond the grave in search of a crime and a killer. Does that whet your appetite? Then turn the page and look for clues. Accept this preface as your retainer, and join in Sleuths, Ltd.'s investigation of *The Case of the Frozen Scream.*

Contents

CHAPTER 1

The Chrome Bone

Intense chill gripped the night air as wisps of fog, swirling, searching, brushed against the window panes. Inside, a blazing fire kept the living room pleasantly warm. It was a perfect evening for curling up with a book—which is exactly what I had done. My partner, however, was waging war across a chess table with our guest, Inspector Twigg. I couldn't help but look up from my reading on occasion to watch the spectacle. Twigg was so methodical—a stocky, bear of a man, slowly contemplating every move. Geoffrey Weston, however, hovered over the board like some half-starved bird of prey ready to swoop down on an unsuspecting victim. The Inspector's hand would hardly release his man before Geoffrey's slim fingers had lifted a bishop or a rook nearly two feet off the table and slammed it down on another square. All that was missing was the "Aha! Now I've got you." Geoffrey's style was intimidating, to say the least.

Finally the Inspector had had enough of it. He looked up from the game and began sipping a cup of hot chocolate.

"Weston," he observed, "you're the most disgustingly unorthodox player I've ever met. I wish some client would barge in here and put an end to your kamikaze raids. Vent your hostilities on some murderer, man, not on me!"

Geoffrey leaned back in his chair and smiled. He tossed a captured queen into the air and caught it before answering.

"I assure you, old fellow, I'd like nothing better than that. But consulting detectives aren't exactly in demand this month. It looks like you'll have to be my target—unless the Yard has a case or two they'd like to throw in my direction."

Twigg set his cup down on the edge of the table.

"As a matter of fact," he volunteered, "we *are* looking into a matter that you might find interesting. It's one of the strangest mysteries—"

"Jolly good," I interrupted, nearly convulsed with laughter. I couldn't hold it in a moment longer. Even Geoffrey struggled to suppress a howl. Inspector Twigg looked at the two of us in bewilderment.

"Are both of you daft? What did I say?"

Geoffrey, clearly losing his battle for composure, took a deep breath and wiped his eyes with a handkerchief.

"Twigg," he chuckled, "you're . . . for a Scotland Yarder you're not overly subtle."

"Not subtle? What on earth do you—"

"I mean," my partner continued, "that you always think of these unusual cases when you're losing—never when you're winning. You wouldn't be trying to distract me, would you?"

Twigg shifted uneasily in his chair before assuming an attitude of mock innocence.

"Why," he protested with a twinkle in his eye, "how ever could you think a thing like that? Just because my story cost you a queen last Tuesday, that's no reason to—"

"Reason enough," I disagreed, "considering the nature of that story! 'How could the wheelchair bandit have entered Garths of Fleet Street through a third-floor window?' After we spent half an hour inventing hoists to push the poor paralytic through, there you sat as dead-pan as an owl—never letting on that the rascal had two good legs and simply stole wheelchairs!"

The Inspector took another sip of hot chocolate, futilely trying to look insulted.

"John Taylor, you amaze me. You and your theatrical friend jump—as usual—to a conclusion. Then you have the temerity to blame me for your own outrageous theories! But," he added with a grin, "I recognize your limitations. And I forgive you—this once."

"Very decent of you," Weston replied with more than a touch of irony. "Now what about this *new* 'case'? Is it another 'Twigg gambit,' or does it have substance?"

The Inspector milked the moment for everything it was worth. He drained his cup and glanced around the room in search of the customary jar of peanuts. As usual every ledge was strewn with books, papers, and laboratory equipment. The prize eluded him.

"Weston, if you really want to know—"

"Of course I want to know, man! Get on with it."

"If you really want to know," Twigg repeated with exasperating deliberateness, "it's a corker! Three nights ago there was a break-in at—of all places—Brompton Cemetery. An alarm sounded in the crematorium shortly after midnight. By the time we got there the crematory was fired up. And when it cooled off enough for us to have a look inside, all we found was a pile of ashes and a chrome-steel hip joint."

"A novel way to dispose of a body," Geoffrey mused. "I presume you've had time to trace the bone to its late owner."

"We have," Twigg confirmed. "Or at least I think we have. It couldn't belong to anyone else. But then it couldn't be his either."

"By which you mean?"

"I mean, Geoff, that the man has an alibi for his own murder! He's disappeared, to be sure. But he was last seen nearly four hours *after* we pulled his joint out of the ashes."

Weston stroked his goatee thoughtfully. His interest was obviously aroused.

"You're certain about that trace?"

"Absolutely," the Inspector asserted. "It hasn't been all that long since the man shattered his hip, and his post-operative X rays were still on file. You're aware, of course, that surgeons grind down pins and sockets to fit the patient. They're almost as distinctive as fingerprints."

"Quite," Geoffrey agreed. "I believe the patient gets ground a might also, but that's beside the point. Now what about that alibi you mentioned? I'd like a few details."

"The victim's name," Twigg began, "is James Chester. He's a professor at Regal College. And it would seem that he's a most determined one. The morning following his cremation no less than four students saw him sitting at his desk busily grading papers. His office window is right next to a sidewalk and they could hardly miss noticing him as they passed. He was due to give a lecture at one o'clock, but evidently even Chester's dedication has some limits. He didn't show up."

"I take it you've investigated the witnesses' backgrounds?"

"We have. And there's virtually no evidence of collusion. As far as we can determine, they really saw what they said they saw. One of them even took—and passed—a polygraph test."

"Fascinating," Weston admitted. "You may really have something this time. Did the victim sport a beard or perhaps a mustache?"

"No, he didn't. He was clean-shaven—even wore his hair close cut."

"How old was he?"

"Fortyish."

At this point I broke into the conversation.

"You realize," I volunteered, "that forty is a dangerous age. Men often get bored with their job and with the routine nature of family life."

"Not this man," Twigg disagreed with conviction. "Chester seemed to revel in his work. And he had been married only two years. If you'd met his wife, you wouldn't think it likely he faked death in order to run off somewhere.

"I take it," Geoffrey remarked, "that this Mrs. Chester is to be our client."

"Quite possibly," the Inspector mused. "I told her how you two handled the Arthur Heath case, and she was quite impressed. If you give a decent presentation—"

"I don't like to be suspicious," my colleague interrupted. "But why are you—if you'll excuse the pun—throwing us this bone? Scotland Yard has never acted as our agent before. In fact, I've sometimes gotten the impression that we weren't particularly appreciated. Clients tend to pull you into our living room—not the reverse."

The Inspector met Geoffrey's gaze and paused.

"I was afraid you'd ask that."

He stood up and walked over to the fireplace, his attention riveted on the Rembrandt print over the mantel, "Christ on the Road to Emmaus."

"You and John," he continued ruefully, "will probably have another good laugh at my expense. But I'll be frank anyway. One Inspector Filbert Twigg is in charge of this investigation, and I don't think he's competent to lead it. He has a—"

"Don't say that," I objected. "There's no other detective on the force more dependable than you are in matters of—"

"John," Twigg insisted, "please let me finish. I know my own strengths and weaknesses. More importantly, I am aware of the limitations that being a Scotland Yarder places upon me." He turned to face us. "I'm not saying I agree with the stunts or the leaps in logic you chaps seem to find so essential. I may never recommend 'Sleuths, Ltd.'—as you call it—to anyone else. But I feel deep down inside that this case is right for you. Will you take it?"

"As long as Mrs. Chester is in agreement," Geoffrey assured him, "I don't see why not."

"Good."

"But," my partner added, "I would like some further explanation for this unexpected humility. From the way you looked at that picture, I gather . . ." His hand suddenly rose to his forehead in a gesture of understanding. "Oh, of course! How stupid of me not to see it. You think James Chester's alibi was *supernatural.* His being seen grading papers was some sort of resurrection! No. . . . Knowing you, you'd probably lean toward something less biblical. A spectre . . . That's it. And you don't want to be laughed out of the Department. So we're going to be your ghost chasers while you make the usual dull, proper, safe entries in your report!"

"Something like that," the Inspector admitted. "Do you mind?"

"Not at all," Weston replied. "But I assure you that we'll be hunting demons rather than ghosts *if* natural explanations prove impossible. And there are a number of very normal solutions that seem far more probable to me right now than your theory. You're usually so earth-bound in your thinking, Twigg. Level-leafed, roots in the soil and all that . . . What ever induced you to go out on a limb?"

"I'll ignore those puns," the Inspector grimaced. "Actually it's the bad company I've been keeping. And I shall rectify that mistake in a moment."

"I'm sure you shall," Geoffrey commented. "But while John fetches your coat, I have a final question or two."

"You usually do."

"What precisely did James Chester teach? And when might I have a talk with the witnesses?"

"Professor Chester," Twigg replied matter-of-factly, "is or was a psychologist—of the behaviorist school, I believe. He taught our future leaders how to train rats. As to the witnesses, how about ten-thirty tomorrow morning?"

"You can't make that any earlier?"

"I could," Twigg rejoined, "but you'd find the schedule a bit tight." He extracted a notebook from his hip pocket. "You are due to meet with Ruth Chester at . . . let me see . . . nine o'clock. Here's her address." He tore out a sheet and handed it to Weston.

"Awfully sure of yourself, weren't you?"

"No," Twigg corrected with the hint of a smile, "I was sure of you. Now, John, if you'll be good enough to hand me my coat. Thank you."

As I helped the Inspector slide his arms into the sleeves, Geoffrey carefully folded the piece of paper and deposited it in his wallet. He would keep the appointment. But he wasn't quite ready to end the conversation.

"Twigg, by tomorrow I want a spectrographic analysis of the hip jont. Compare your findings with the manufacturer's records and let me know if it's the same metal."

"Done."

"And I want a profile on the witnesses."

"That," the Inspector declared, "will take a little longer."

"Give me the information as soon as you have it."

"Fair enough."

We shook hands all around and made our way across the room, skirting some boxes and a telescope. Bachelor flats have a way of collecting odds and ends. I opened the door for our guest, and he stepped into the swirling fog. As his footsteps grew fainter in the distance, Geoffrey made a megaphone of his hands.

"By the way, old fellow . . . Checkmate in three moves!"

Twigg didn't answer.

* * * * *

We stood for several moments staring into the night. The ghostly glow of the street lamp filtered through the mist, and a passing bobby pointed his torch at us. Aside from that there was only darkness. The brownstones across the street might have been a hundred miles distant for all we saw of them. I shivered and turned away. Weston closed the door with a bang.

"It is a mite nippy," he agreed.

I retraced my steps toward the warmth and security of the fireside.

"I wasn't merely shivering from the cold," I confessed. "It's a dismal evening to be talking about demons." I stood in front of the dancing flames, rubbing my hands together.

"Not as dismal for us as for Twigg," Weston ventured. "He wouldn't admit it, but I think he's afraid. Remember he was standing right in the room when devils surfaced in the Heath case. And he knows he's defenseless!" Geoffrey sat down in his easy chair and fished a jar of peanuts from off the carpet.

"The man's an enigma," I complained. "He was so close to surrendering to Jesus that evening. But since then . . ."

"He's still close," my partner disagreed solemnly. "But he's trying to brace himself against the pull. We'll simply have to keep praying."

I sighed and switched on the stereo. The cheerful strains of a Stolz waltz began to ebb and flow in the background. "Die ganze Welt ist himmelblau." I recognized the melody. But at the moment the world seemed anything but the "heavenly blue" that the title suggested.

"Weston, why did you dismiss the idea of a spectre as out of hand?"

My colleague looked at me strangely.

"Because, old fellow, there are no such things as ghosts."

"Of course there aren't in the popular sense," I agreed with a touch of embarrassment. "But I once read a claim by J. B. Phillips that C. S. Lewis appeared to him shortly after death. Couldn't a person's spirit be allowed to linger a few days before going to heaven or hell?"

Geoffrey propped his chin up with an arm. He paused a long moment before replying.

"As I remember the story, John, C. S. Lewis appeared to Phillips and then *reappeared* a week later. That's an awfully long linger! And Christians like Lewis have the promise that absence from the body means presence with the Lord."

"But," I pointed out, "God's presence isn't limited to heaven. He might give the man a hug, so to speak, but keep him on earth a few days."

"I suppose that's possible," Geoffrey conceded. "But I think it highly unlikely—and a special case if it did happen. The Scriptures never mention a gap. It's more likely that Phillips either suffered from a delusion or that Lewis returned from heaven on an errand."

"Something like Samuel's confrontation of Saul?"

"Yes. I believe God intervened for a special reason there. The witch of Endor tried to contact a demon but got a prophet. At least a return from paradise or heaven has some biblical precedent. A lingering ghost has virtually none!"

"Well then," I reflected, "we still might have James Chester's disembodied spirit making an appearance."

"Not at all." Weston tossed some peanuts into his mouth. "You see, John, God never does anything without good reason. He's created an orderly world built around principles of cause and effect. Without that we'd be out of business. Clues wouldn't mean anything. They wouldn't be clues."

"But what has that got to do with—"

"It has everything to do with it. God doesn't play games. He doesn't deal in nonsense. He does not glorify the pointless. Look at the case of Samuel. Saul was running roughshod over the nation—perverting an entire generation. Then he had the gall to delve into the occult. With brilliant irony God gave the rascal what he wanted—a talk with Samuel. And Samuel pronounced judgment on the man. Now let's look at the case of C. S. Lewis—if it's a real case. J. B. Phillips is a successful Bible translator. But he's going through a difficult period in his life. Phillips has corresponded with Lewis and respects him. So Lewis appears and gives the gentleman an important personal message. That makes sense, too, doesn't it?"

"Certainly," I agreed, "but I still don't see—"

"John, don't be dense. Look at this strange Chester affair. The man is presumably seen after his death. Does he have a message to give anyone? No. Is there any logical reason that God would send him? No. All the man does is grade a few papers . . . continue the daily routine . . . waste a few moments on the trivial. The incident doesn't ring true at all. And, of course, we don't even know that the man was a Christian. If not, he would be confined in escape-proof facilities I assure you. Even if he were a Christian, he surely wouldn't leave the lap of luxury in order to perform some pointless scholastic ritual. No, my friend, God did not allow James Chester's 'ghost' to walk the halls of Regal College. We are dealing here with either delusion, illusion, collusion, demonic impersonation, or . . ."

"Or what?"

"Or a man who isn't dead at all."

I turned the volume up on the stereo and went to the kitchen to brew a fresh pot of tea. We'd know soon enough what we were up against. And for now I was content to await hard evidence—and to relax. When I returned with the cups, Geoffrey already had his nose in a book.

CHAPTER 2

Two or More Witnesses

Our motorcar escaped the heavy traffic of Brompton Road and glided to a halt on a side street. It was nine o'clock on the button. The bungalow before us looked out of place—its stucco walls contrasting with the red brick that dominated Edgerton Terrace.

As we approached the veranda I marveled at the well-groomed shrubbery. Each bush was a meticulous little green package still wet with morning dew. Centered on the door was a brass plate, inscribed simply "The Chesters."

"Who do you think," I wondered aloud, "is the fanatic for order? This place is rather like a storybook house."

"Probably the wife," Weston observed. "A man would hardly paint a building pink. We'd best get about our business before someone accuses us of nibbling on the steps."

My colleague managed only a single knock before the door opened inward. Ruth Chester had been expecting us. At once I saw why Twigg had been impressed. The woman was a stately blond—tall and slender with classic Roman features. Although she seemed composed, her grey-blue eyes revealed a trace of tragedy.

"Good morning, gentlemen." Her voice was deep and resonant. She looked from one to the other of us. "I presume that one of you is Mr. Weston."

"I am," Geoffrey acknowledged. "At your service." He pulled a card from his pocket and presented it to her. Mrs. Chester glanced briefly at the writing:

Sleuths, Ltd.
London's Consulting Detective Firm
Number 31, Baker Street

"And this rotund fellow," Geoffrey continued, "is my partner, John Taylor, Esq. You may be assured of both his competence and his integrity."

"I'm sure of that," she acknowledged with a forced smile. "Will you please come in."

We followed her into a Danish modern living room. Plastic flowed, chrome gleamed, and not so much as a paper clip was out of place. Many would have considered the arrangement fashionable. But it seemed rather cold to me—and inhuman. I half expected a robot to roll out of the closet and sweep the floor after us. Mrs. Chester gestured toward two molded buckets. We sat down and waited for her to open the conversation. When she did, her voice quivered slightly.

"Mr. Weston, Inspector Twigg has probably given you some details about the . . . the disappearance."

"Yes, he has."

She seated herself on the sofa and brushed her hair back over her shoulders.

"Have you any idea yet as to what may have happened?"

"Five or six hypotheses seem attractive," Geoffrey began optimistically. "But there's not enough information yet to—"

"I quite understand," she interrupted. "At least you hold out some hope of finding my husband or his murderer."

"Most certainly," Geoffrey assured her. "The case is bizarre, but I believe it can be solved. And John and I intend to do just that."

Ruth Chester opened her mouth to speak but then hesitated. She compressed her lips, considering her next move. Finally, reaching over to the glass coffee table, the woman rummaged through her purse and extracted a bulging envelope.

"I've read about your exploits in the *Times*, Mr. Weston," she said decisively, "and I do not believe the Inspector made a mistake in recommending you. You should find this sufficient as a retainer. If you bring matters to a successful conclusion, I am prepared to give you an additional three thousand pounds." She handed the envelope to Geoff who in turn passed it on to me.

"That will be quite satisfactory," he acknowledged. "John will give you a receipt before we leave. Now, if it's not too much bother, I'd like to ask you a few questions."

"Of course. I suppose that's part of what I'm paying for."

"It is, indeed. And I'd appreciate it if you would answer each question just as candidly as possible."

She nodded her assent, shifting position tensely.

"Mrs. Chester, I understand you've been married about two years. How long did you know your husband before that?"

Hesitating a second before answering, she closed her eyes—as if trying to look back into time. Her fingers moved slightly as she counted to herself.

"Exactly three months and seventeen days, Mr. Weston. I was a student in one of his classes. And Jim was . . . is a very charming man. We had somewhat of a whirlwind courtship."

"Did he walk with a limp?"

"No. I didn't even know about his problem until after we were married."

"How long ago," Geoffrey inquired, "did the operation take place?"

"It's been over four years now. I can't say exactly when. Jim didn't talk about it. He was rather sensitive to the difference in our ages, and . . . well, he always wanted me to think of him as young and dashing. He isn't a vain man, Mr. Weston, but he . . . he even worries about the grey streaks in his hair."

"Did he have any hobbies?"

"Only golf. He was an avid golfer."

"Now think carefully before you answer," my partner cautioned. "Was there anyone—to your knowledge—who would have reason to kill your husband? Did he have any enemies?"

A tear began to trickle down Ruth Chester's cheek, belying the stoic set of her face.

"Jim was . . . is very outgoing and friendly. Everybody likes him. He even counsels with students when he has a chance. It's not required. He just cares about people."

"I'm sure he does," Geoffrey acknowledged. "But even nice chaps are known to step on a few toes now and then."

"I suppose so," she admitted. "But Jim is something special."

"And you're in love with him."

Ruth Chester lowered her eyes and gazed at her hands.

"Yes, I am. You're right, of course, to doubt my judgment."

"Not so much your judgment," I spoke out compassionately, "as your opportunity to see the whole truth. Geoffrey and I have observed people in all sorts of situations. And even the best man or woman has a hatful of rolls to play. A wife may witness only one side of her husband's character."

"There are very few closets without skeletons," Weston added. "Some men are simply adept at exhibiting their Dr. Jekyll and hiding Mr. Hyde."

"And some men," Ruth Chester rebutted in tearful disgust, "are cynics."

Geoffrey looked at her keenly before replying. When he spoke it was with an odd mixture of annoyance and tenderness.

"I prefer to think of myself, Madam, as a realist. There's a rottenness in man. If that weren't so, your husband wouldn't be in the business of patching up shattered psyches. If that weren't so, England wouldn't have a legacy of half-empty churches while self-help quackery sells like discounted crumpets on every bookrack. Lady Macbeth isn't the only one who curses bloody hands while rubbing them with useless soap in hopes of purity. We've forgotten the promises of the Reformation and are busily trying to reform ourselves!"

Mrs. Chester straightened her skirt, pulling it down over her knees.

"That may be so, Mr. Weston. I'm sorry I insulted you." She paused to blow her nose before continuing. "Please excuse my lack of composure, gentlemen. I'm ready for the rest of your questions now, and I'll try not to be emotional."

"There is no apology necessary," Geoffrey assured her. "I quite understand the strain you're under." He paused briefly to recapture his train of thought and then went on quickly. "When was the last time you saw James?"

She answered in a slow, steady voice—almost a monotone.

"It was the morning before that awful crematory was turned on. Jim walked to the college as usual, but . . . but he never came home."

"Did anyone at the school see him?"

"Oh, yes. He taught his classes as usual and left his office at about four o'clock. One of the students noticed him walking toward the edge of the campus."

Weston leaned forward in his chair and pointed a boney finger at her.

"Now this is important. On a scale of one to ten, how do you think James rated your marriage for excitement."

"You sound just like him," Mrs. Chester reminisced. "He often gave tests like that. He—"

"Answer the question," Weston demanded.

"About a . . . about a six—maybe a seven."

My colleague drummed his fingers on the side of the chair.

"Have there been any large withdrawals from your bank account recently?"

"No. Inspector Twigg had me call up and make an inquiry."

"Good for him," Geoffrey complimented. "That's enough cross examination for today. If you'll just draw a sketch of Jim's route to work, we'll be on our way.

Weston rose to his feet, and the two of us followed suit.

"I will return tomorrow," he informed her. "When I do, I want all of your husband's business papers ready for my inspection. And, oh yes, go through your library and divide the books into two piles—yours and his. Does James by any chance keep rat cages or the like at home?"

Ruth Chester smiled the first genuine smile of our visit.

"Mr. Weston," she admitted, "he wouldn't dare."

My colleague and I shook hands with our client. She sketched the crude map that Geoffrey wanted, and I gave her a receipt for her retainer. Soon we were outside once again walking toward our motorcar. The sky was overcast and a slow but steady rain had begun to fall. But Geoffrey didn't seem disturbed in the least.

"John, I think I'll take a stroll to the college. Why don't you meet me at Chester's office."

"Twigg's expecting us shortly," I reminded him.

"And he shall have us. But I want to have a look around before this drizzle gets any heavier. One may count on Filbert for the obvious. He's undoubtedly asked around the neighborhood for witnesses to an abduction. But he may not have combed the grass."

I was horrified.

"Good grief, man! That will take hours."

"I'll try," my partner replied tongue-in-cheek, "to only comb the bald spots."

Without another word, he pulled the magnifier out of his overcoat pocket and began walking slowly up the street. His eyes never left the ground. I shrugged and opened the door to our Mercedes. Conversations with Geoffrey tended to end rather abruptly. In a matter of seconds I was driving toward Regal College—my whistling accompanied by the steady "thump, thump" of the wiper blades.

* * * * *

The college had grown substantially since my last visit, back in the seventies. As I hunted for a parking space, I noticed a score of new buildings that hadn't been there before. Imposing old granite structures were now surrounded by cookie-cutter classroom buildings and an occasional wood frame cottage. After some delay I found a place to park and made a dash for the nearest shelter. A student there told me where I could find

Dr. Chester's domain. Fortunately it was only one building away in one of those wooden "temporaries."

As I approached at a full run, I saw Inspector Twigg standing in the doorway. He spied me at the same instant and called out a greeting.

"Well, well. Here comes a whale of a detective. Where's your skinny friend?"

I stepped into the vestibule before answering.

"He'll be along in a few minutes, Twigg. Stop blubbering and let's get down to business."

The Inspector groaned.

"Touché, old chap. You're starting to sound like Weston."

"Purely a matter of survival," I assured him. "Now where are the witnesses?"

"I've got them packed away in the room next to Chester's. And I can tell you they're not happy about it. All three are missing classes."

"How times have changed," I mused. "When I was in school we liked nothing better than to weedle an excused absence."

"How right you are!"

As we walked down the corridor the Inspector—now all business—acted as my tour guide.

"As you can see, John, there are exits at both ends of this building. For reasons of safety these doors open freely from the inside. The custodian and a whole bevy of instructors have keys to the outside locks."

"The entire building is used for office space?"

"Except for the room across from Chester's office. That's where he conducts his experiments. All told there are nine offices and the laboratory—five rooms to a side."

"And every one," I wagered, "will be equally drab."

Twigg nodded.

"That's the nature of 'temporaries,' isn't it? And they'll be drabber still in fifty years. Chester's office is down there on the end. Here's our door."

We entered a dingy room dominated by a scarred wooden desk, four straight-backed chairs, and an equal number of very bored university students. The young lady in the group looked up from her magazine.

"Inspector. We've been waiting here for twenty minutes. When are we going to be able to leave?"

"I assure you," Twigg consoled her, "that it won't be long now."

"It 'ad betta not be," a fellow in the corner retorted nasally. He had the build of a jockey but the broken nose and course manner of a fighter. "I 'ave a date fo' lunch. And she'd neva believe I was 'elpin' the Yard."

"Relax," Twigg replied. "You might not be any help at all."

"Very funny, very funny. You're a regula constable comedian. That's what *you* are."

"I'll ignore that, Singleton," the Inspector warned, "but if you open your mouth again to do anything but answer questions, you'll be here until this case is closed."

"Aw go on."

The young man waved his hand in derision. But he fell silent.

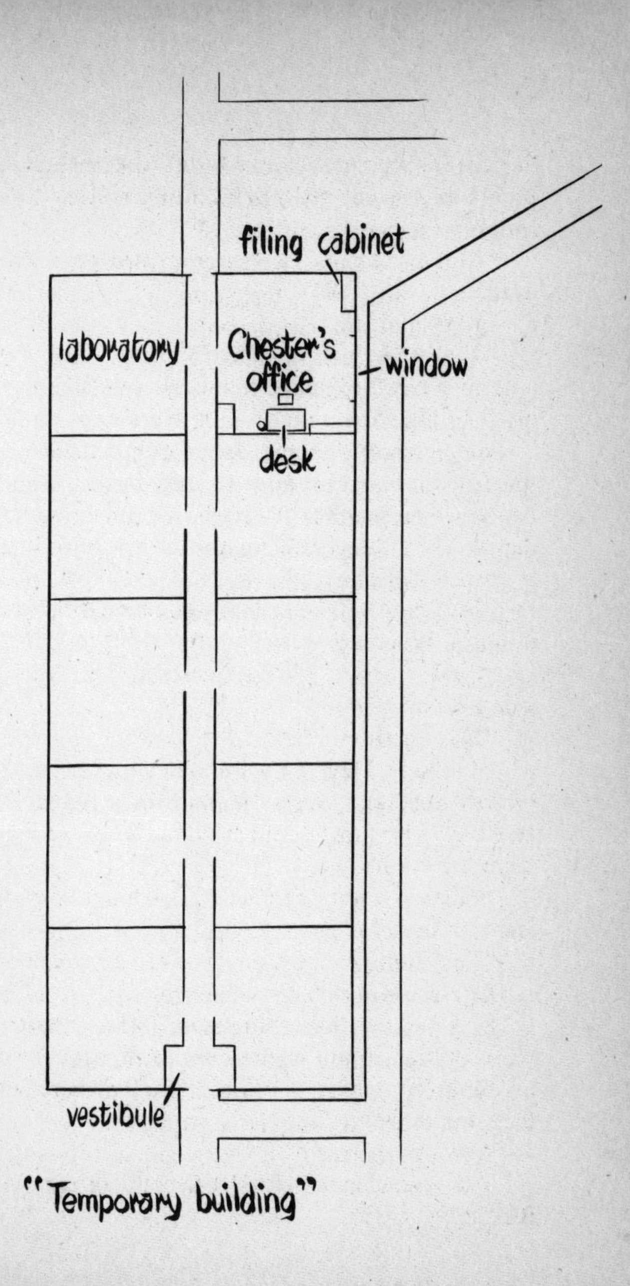

"Temporary building"

"We might as well get on with the preliminaries," I suggested, "before Geoffrey arrives. That should speed things up a bit."

"As you wish," Twigg acknowledged. "That gentleman with the sharp tongue over there is George Singleton. He doesn't usually look like he's eaten an unripe banana—only when he's awake. And the athletic fellow by the window is Stephen Hill."

Stephen nodded a greeting. His blond hair was thinning a mite on top, and although sloppily dressed, he was quite handsome. I jotted down the names as the Inspector spoke.

"And the dark-skinned scholar with the spectacles is Chad Johnson. It's his first year here, so he hasn't gotten lazy yet."

Chad looked up from his textbook and grinned.

"Pleased to meet you, Mr. . . . "

"Taylor," I replied. "John Taylor."

"Pleased to meet you, I'm sure. I hope you can find the professor."

"The young lady," Twigg concluded, "is Sandra Meyer. Don't be fooled by the silky hair and soulful eyes. She has a chance of graduating summa cum laude."

Sandra rewarded the Inspector with a radiant smile. She was a petite, pretty brunette with dimples—and evidently well aware of the fact.

"Well," I ventured, "now that we've concluded with the introductions, let's proceed."

At that moment Geoffrey stepped through the door. Water was still dripping off his coat, his shoes were a muddy mess, and he had the general appearance of a drowned pelican.

"Weston," Twigg remarked, "it's about time you arrived. What on earth have you been doing—digging up clues in a hog wallow?"

"As a matter of fact," Weston responded ruefully, "I've been out finding a new penny, a nineteen-twelve farthing, two buttons, and a handful of bent nails."

The Inspector chuckled in spite of himself.

"That will just about pay your cleaning bills—that is, if you BEAT the dirt out with a rock."

Geoffrey slipped off his shoes, and I helped him shed his coat. Standing there in a turtle-neck sweater, slacks and stocking feet, he didn't look very professional, but he was ready to get down to work. I gave him the list of names. He gazed intently at each of the students before speaking.

"I'm terribly sorry to have inconvenienced you," he apologized. "But then a man's life may hang in the balance. If you're harboring any resentment at being brought here, please take a deep breath and calm down. Angry people aren't clear thinkers, and you're going to have to give clear, accurate answers. Mr. Hill, will you begin by telling us your version of what happened?"

Stephen Hill shrugged and looked Geoffrey straight in the eye.

"There isn't very much to tell, really. I was on my way to a microbiology lecture when I passed this building. I looked in the window to Professor Chester's office and saw him sitting at his desk grading papers."

"Was the window open?" my partner prompted.

"Yes. It was a warm day. I remember being pleasantly surprised that morning that I wouldn't have to bundle up."

"You were coming from what class?"

"From home, Mr. . . . "

"Weston. Geoffrey Weston."

Stephen Hill crossed his legs and smiled disarmingly. He was clearly enjoying being the center of attention.

"Microbiology, Mr. Weston, is the first class on my schedule. As it happens I arrived that day a trifle early—at about a quarter to eleven. I remember looking at my watch as I walked into the room—surprised that the place was so empty. Let me see . . . Figuring travel time, that would put me outside Chester's window at—give or take a minute—ten forty-two. That's what you want to know, isn't it?"

Geoffrey eyed the young man up and down from his neatly combed hair to his well-worn jeans and tennis shoes. My partner was impressed by alertness when he saw it.

"Yes, Mr. Hill, that's what I wanted to know. You didn't by any chance say a word or two to the chap as you passed, did you?"

"No," Stephen admitted. "Dr. Chester seemed so engrossed in what he was doing I didn't want to be a bother. He was puffing away on that cigar of his and working his way through a stack of papers."

"Did he wave to you?"

"No. I doubt he even saw me."

"And his color . . . did it look natural?"

"As well as anyone's could through a cloud of smoke."

"How long," Geoffrey inquired, "was that cigar?"

Stephen held up his thumb and forefinger as if using them to measure what he had seen.

"Let me think now. I believe . . . yes, it must have been about four inches long—almost new."

"Could you smell the smoke?"

The student hesitated.

"I'm not sure about that. I don't usually remember smells. But there may have been a somewhat sweet odor."

My partner stroked his goatee in thought.

"Thank you, Mr. Hill. You may go now."

Stephen Hill seemed surprised that the questioning was over so quickly. He disentangled himself from the chair and left the room uncertainly—as though he half expected to be called back. As his footsteps receded down the hall, Geoffrey turned to another witness.

"Miss . . . Meyer, will you please tell us now about your experience."

Sandra Meyer tilted her head coquettishly and looked at Geoffrey with a seriousness that almost amounted to a pout. Her voice was so soft I had to strain to hear.

"I'm afraid I can't be of much help," she apologized. "I saw exactly the same things Mr. Hill described."

"Exactly?"

"Well, I didn't smell any smoke. But I saw the man sitting there in front of a pile of papers and puffing that four-inch smoke stack." She crinkled up her nose in disgust. "I feel polluted every time I get near a smoker. It's a disgusting habit, don't you agree?"

"Quite," Geoffrey responded.

He paced the length of the room—then turned to address her again.

"Would you say the lighting was good enough so you can be sure it was really Chester you saw?"

"Oh, most certainly. It was kind of dim inside, but he had a desk lamp lit and it shone right on his face."

"I'd like to get a clear picture of the time frame," Weston confided. "Can you give me a rough idea of when you passed by the window?"

"I can do better than that. I was late for class. The church clock chimed the hour just before I saw the chap."

"By the hour you mean?"

"Eleven o'clock, of course."

"I have one last question and then you may go," Geoffrey promised. "Was the office window open or closed?"

"I think . . . Let me try to picture the scene. I think it was . . . open. But that doesn't make much sense, does it? I would have smelled the smoke. It must have been—"

"Thank you for your help, Miss Meyer," Weston interrupted. "You may leave now if you wish."

"You don't want to—"

"No, that will be quite enough, thank you."

Sandra Meyer was not happy at being cut off in the middle of a sentence. But she shook hands with my colleague anyway and left the room. She would have seemed more wholesome if she had removed the wiggle from her walk.

"Now, gentlemen," Weston continued, "we seem to be down to two." He glanced at the list of names. "Which of you is Mr. Singleton and which is Chad Johnson?"

"I'm George Singleton." The uncouth chap in the corner glared at us as if daring us to claim he wasn't. "And I don't 'ave nothin' ta say what 'asn't already been said."

"Is that so," Geoffrey mused. "Was the door in Chester's office open or closed when you passed?"

"It was . . . closed. Yes, closed . . . I'm sure of it."

"And you, Mr. Singleton, walked by at what time?"

"Why it was right after class let out. Couldn't 'ave been more than a minute. I 'ad a lecture in the buildin' right next ta this. Me and Chad 'ere was walkin' together, we was."

"That's right, Mr. Weston," Chad Johnson agreed. "We got to our next class on time, so it must have been at eight or nine of that we saw the professor. My next class was on the other side of campus, and we only have ten minute breaks."

"And 'e was just sittin' there," George volunteered, "big as life—puffin' away and breakin' some poor students' 'earts with 'is red pencil."

Geoffrey gazed out of the window for a few seconds. I could almost hear the gears turning in his mind. Then he glanced in turn at George Singleton and at his swarthy companion.

"Did either of you say anything to James Chester?"

"I did," Chad recalled, "but he didn't answer. I don't think he heard."

"And did either of you smell smoke?"

The two looked at each other and then shook their heads in the negative.

"I can't remember any," Johnson confirmed. He began chewing the end of his glasses. "The window may have been closed."

"Are you in the habit," Geoffrey remarked, "of talking to people through closed windows?"

"No, of course not. I mean—"

"And you, Mr. Singleton, did you happen to notice the style and size of the cigar?"

"It was kind o' plump—if ya know what I mean. But I 'aven't the foggiest 'ow long it was. Old Chester wasn't missin' then and there wasn't much reason ta notice details."

"Quite right," my partner agreed. "You've done well to remember what you have."

"I think it was on the long side," Chad recollected. "But I'm not sure."

Geoffrey fixed Chad Johnson with his gaze.

"He was sitting so you had a side view of him at the window?"

"Yes. That's right."

"Was it overcast or sunny outside?"

"Definitely sunny. That's why we had our coats off."

"Windy?"

"Not so you'd notice."

Weston paused.

"Have either of you two gentlemen ever undergone psychological counseling?"

"Now look 'ere," Singleton flashed, "there ain't nobody what's goin' to get away with sayin' we was seein' things."

"Answer my question," Geoffrey demanded.

George Singleton's face flashed in anger. I could see his jaw muscles tighten. My partner was at least a head taller and had a two stone weight advantage, but I thought for a second the miniature scarecrow was going to attack. Instead, however, he broke eye contact and glanced downward in . . . it looked like embarrassment!

"I was seein' Professor Chester sort of regular. But it was nothin' serious, you understand. I just have this little problem with my temper."

"We've noticed," Geoffrey replied sardonically.

"And I wasn't the only one, neither. Did you see 'ow Stephen 'ill was always standin' by the window? The professor was trying to cure 'is claustrophobia. I guess that's why the two o' us noticed Chester when we passed. 'e means somethin' to us."

"I suppose," my partner mused. "Did either Chad or Sandra ever—"

"I certainly didn't," Chad Johnson declared. "I don't have a problem in the world, and I'm not about to be psychoanalyzed by anyone."

"No, I don't think you would," Weston reflected. "That, gentlemen, should pretty well wind things up. If I need to meet with you further, I'll get in touch. Good day and have a nice afternoon."

The two students gathered their textbooks together and—with evident relief—headed toward the hallway. I picked up Geoffrey's coat and shoes in anticipation of our own departure. But as George Singleton turned to wave a "cheerio" to the Inspector, Weston got in one final shot.

"By the way, George, I almost forgot. Did your treatment by Professor Chester ever involve the use of hypnosis?"

"It did not!" he fairly bellowed.

Singleton slammed the door and stomped angrily down the hall.

The Inspector buttoned his trench coat matter-of-factly.

"It's amazing," he observed, "the way you put people at ease. Who was your charm school teacher? The hunchback of Notre Dame or Atilla the Hun?"

"There are times," Geoffrey responded, "when hard questions have to be asked. And this was one of them. I feel very ill at ease about what these witnesses said."

"You and everyone else," Twigg agreed. "What's next on your agenda?"

"John and I will be having a look at that notorious office. If you'll be good enough to let us in, we'll take matters from there. By the way, I assume it was Sandra Meyer who took the polygraph test."

"How did you know?"

"The others were hardly likely candidates, old fellow. I don't suppose you could get her to agree to questioning under sodium pentathol?"

"About as much chance as the Nazis have of winning a majority in Parliament."

"I was afraid of that," my partner conceded. "It certainly would be a help, but I guess we can muddle through on another track."

"You think they're lying?"

Geoffrey sighed and opened the door that Singleton had slammed.

"I think that they did not see what they say they saw or that they saw something other than what they thought they saw."

"That's about as clear as a fog bank."

"Isn't it though. You may lead the way to the good professor's inner sanctum."

Turning right we headed toward the end of the hall—Geoffrey still in his stocking feet. As we walked, I marvelled at the ugliness of the place. The walls were a depressing grey—no doubt to cut down on cleaning bills. And the passageway was far too narrow to suit my taste. Everything was bare and institutional. Stopping in front of the last door on the right, Twigg began fumbling through his keys.

"I'll open up the laboratory too," he volunteered. "But please be good sports and make sure both rooms are secure before you leave."

"I am aware of the procedure," Weston commented dryly. "I assume you've done *your* part in keeping things undisturbed."

"We have," the Inspector assured us. "The

windows have been closed to keep out the weather, but aside from that . . . "

"What about the custodian?" I inquired. "Did he do any cleaning between the afternoon preceding the crematory episode and your arrival on the scene?"

Twigg waved his arm as if displaying the premises.

"Now I ask you, John. Does it look like this place is scrubbed down every twenty-four hours? About all that's ever done is to empty the waste baskets. And not even that has happened recently."

He worked a key into the lock and twisted. The door opened slowly—revealing a very ordinary-looking interior.

"I've advised the caretaker at Brompton Cemetery that you may be dropping in later this afternoon. He'll be expecting you. Now, unless you need any further assistance, I'll be trotting along."

"Trot away," Weston chuckled, "but you'll never qualify for Ascot."

Twigg glared at Geoffrey, unlocked the far door, and walked down the hall with the most dignified stride he could muster. I pulled my partner's magnifying glass out of his coat and deposited both coat and shoes in a neat pile on the floor. We entered James Chester's office and looked about us.

The usual battered desk was shoved against the right-hand wall between a bookcase and a waste basket. Not much originality there! In the corner nearest the doorway, the professor had set up a refreshment table—complete with hot plate, coffee, cocoa and minute soup. The left-hand wall was totally bare except for a large metal filing cabinet in the far corner.

"Well," I observed, "this is hardly the Dorchester. Where do we start?"

Weston relieved me of his glass and paused to consider the austere furnishings.

"John, I'd like you to start with the floor. Take samples of whatever you find, and pay particular attention to the cracks in the floorboards."

He walked over to the desk and switched on the lamp—obviously presuming that the Yard had already dusted for prints. I turned on the overhead light and then—literally—got down to business. It was slow going since I didn't even know what I was searching for. After ten minutes on my hands and knees I had discovered a goodly supply of dust, soil, spilled coffee and some hairs and dandruff which probably belonged to the professor. Meanwhile my partner was busily ransacking the desk.

"I hope you're doing better than I am," I complained.

Geoffrey slammed shut the last of the drawers. He was clearly perplexed.

"That depends, John, on whether the absence of clues is a clue in itself. I'd be very interested in finding those papers Chester was grading."

"What about the cigar ashes?"

"Now that's a brighter spot," Geoffrey conceded. "I've bagged the contents of the ashtray. It looks like the leavings of a single cigar—probably one of medium length."

"And the trash bucket?"

"Contains a generous supply of the same kind of ash. But it's down at the bottom under some dated memos. What's on the desk evidently represents the total output of the man for both the day before and the day after the crematorium break-in."

"You're certain of that?"

"Reasonably," Weston concluded. "Why don't you check the floor over here by the desk. There may be a few more uncrushed ashes lying about. I'll get out of your way."

So saying, my colleague tiptoed over to the bookcase and began pulling out those volumes of interest to him. I worked my way over to the area he'd vacated. The boards were grey with ground-in droppings. But I couldn't find anything recent.

"Nothing here," I reported, "unless you smashed the evidence with your own feet."

"Or," Weston pointed out, "unless Twigg's associates did so. I'm finding Chester's taste in reading rather interesting. He seems to favor agnostics and determinists. But then some of the titles may be publishers' samples. Teachers tend to save even what they despise."

I got back on my feet and stretched the kinks out of my back.

"You should find the filing cabinet to your liking," I predicted. "I'm going to have a look at that snack table."

"Just don't drink anything," Geoffrey advised

with a smile. "It may be poisoned."

"Oh, go on!"

I stepped over to the refreshment stand and—without touching anything—peered closely at the cups. There was a sprinkling of a distinctive dark powder at the base of each. The Yard's fingerprint experts had already done their usual thorough job. I opened the tin of cocoa and sampled it with the tip of my finger. It didn't seem to be adulterated. Neither did the coffee. Meanwhile Weston had gone to the far corner of the room—to one side of the window—and was systematically working his way through file drawers. There wasn't much left for me to do, so I strolled over and joined him.

"This is almost entirely bureaucratic garbage," Geoffrey declared in disgust. He pulled a drawer completely out of the case and handed it to me. "See if you can find anything of value."

I leafed through folders of equipment requisitions, routine lecture notes, delivery receipts, and statistical analyses of every freshman class for the last ten years. Geoff was right. There was very little of substance.

"Here's a day-by-day record of monkey metabolic rates," I volunteered. "Do you want me to pull it for later study?"

"Please," Geoffrey decided. "It may give us a hint as to the man's experiments. Well, that's all for this drawer. Are you about finished?"

"Yes, quite!" I handed him my drawer, and he slid it into the cabinet. But instead of turning away he stared at the structure. Finally—after a long interval—he spoke.

"John, look at the dust."

I ran my finger over the top of the cabinet and it came away clean.

"There isn't any," I puzzled.

"Precisely," Weston declared. "Don't you think that odd?" Without another word he turned and walked out of the room.

It took us only five minutes to inspect the laboratory. It was crammed with animal cages, mazes, Skinner boxes, and other paraphernalia. The highlight of our tour was an isolation booth housing a chimpanzee. Computer buttons inside enabled the chimp to communicate with the outside world and, presumably, to receive rewards. I'd heard of similar experiments where animals built up a vocabulary of two hundred words or more. The chimp seemed well-fed. But he shrieked his dissatisfaction nonetheless as we returned to the hallway and locked up. He may have been sorry to see us leave. But I wasn't.

CHAPTER 3

The Counterfeit Resurrection

Brompton Cemetery was only a few blocks south of Regal College. But the drizzle of the preceding hour had turned into a downpour. Staccato splashes inundated the windshield, and Geoffrey and I both strained forward trying to see the road.

"You'd think," I complained, "that you could pick a better day than this to start an investigation."

"When criminals are unionized," my partner commented dryly, "maybe we can form a detective's cooperative and negotiate better working conditions."

"That would be quite a change for the better," I fantasized—raising my voice above the drum of the rain. "Imagine nine-to-five sleuths tracking nine-to-five hooligans!"

"You forget, old chap, that evil workers love the night. Your 'nine-to-five' would be nine at night to five in the morning."

"Why is it," I chuckled, "that I always get the short end of the stick? Even when I've got the 'union' behind me!"

We were moving ahead at little more than a

crawl. But in spite of that I almost missed the break in the stone wall marking the entrance.

"There it is, Geoff!" I pointed to a spot just beyond. "Over there to the left!"

My partner hit the brakes, barely having time to negotiate the turn. Then, after we pulled into the drive, our engine suddenly stalled. I opened the side window a crack and had a look out. Row on row of gravestones stood at grisly attention on the lawn—overshadowed now and again by the grotesque, bare branches of an elm. Weston opened the door on his side and stepped out into the elements. Gusts of wind blew rain through the open door. After surveying the situation, he bent down towards me and shouted. "There's a church over there built into the wall! I can see a light inside. Want to make a dash for it? The motor's probably drowned by that puddle we went through. We can look under the bonnet when the weather lets up a bit."

"That suits me!"

Opening the door I braced myself against the driving wind and rain. Geoffrey was already several lengths ahead of me, so I started off at a trot, clutching my coat tightly about me as I tried to catch up. There was indeed a church—a solid stone structure that loomed ahead in the gloom of the storm. The glimmer behind the stained glass was so enticing that I made an extra effort and almost came abreast of my partner.

"Do you think there's a back way in?" I cried. "It would be a shame to have to go around the wall to get to the front!"

"Who knows?" Weston managed between breaths. "We'll find out soon enough!"

As we neared the corner of the building a back entrance came into view. Almost winded, I took the stairs two at a time and ran in under the archway. There I leaned against a granite wall and gasped until normal breathing returned. My arms were trembling and covered with goose bumps.

"You're out of condition," Geoffrey bantered. "No more cold woodcock and mince pie for you!"

"I can do without cold anything," I shivered. "Let's go in. Perhaps they've got a heater."

Geoffrey led the way past the door and through a narrow, dimly lit passageway. Our every step made a hollow clicking sound that echoed through the building. One could hardly believe it was only two in the afternoon. It felt like the dead of night. I prayed silently asking for the Lord's protection—and hoping we might be used to unearth whatever evil lay at the root of Chester's disappearance.

Coming out of the passageway we found ourselves next to the side wall to the left of the altar. Electric lights shown brightly. An elderly gentleman in coveralls was in the center aisle singing a hymn off key and mopping the floor. The roof leaked in several places. The sanctuary was airy, damp, and chill.

"Hallo over there," I hailed. "You wouldn't be the caretaker, would you?"

The man looked up at us quickly—quite apparently startled. Then he leaned forward slightly and squinted as though trying to make us out.

"I would for a fact. And who might you be?"

"John Taylor," I identified myself. "And this is my friend Geoffrey Weston. Inspector Twigg said you'd be expecting us Mr. . . ."

"Thompson, Jasper Thompson," he filled in with a shrill voice. "But I wasn't expecting you. Didn't think you'd come in this storm. Just heard it's going to turn to snow by nightfall, it is. Nasty day for man or beast."

He put down the mop and walked over to us. Jasper, I could see, was no stranger to work. Thick arms and calloused hands showed as much. He was a craggy man with a shock of curly white hair on top that seemed so out of place it was almost a joke.

"You fellows look a little the worse for wear," he noticed. "Maybe you'd like to dry off before taking a peek into the crematorium."

"That," I agreed, "would be just fine."

The two of us followed him to a supply closet where he produced a couple of towels and an umbrella. The towels helped somewhat. Instead of soaked, our clothes were soon upgraded to merely clammy. Hopefully the umbrella would maintain the status quo as we trudged across the field to our destination. As soon as we left the church, however, we were drenched anew.

Jasper led the way through a driving rain. Now resigned to discomfort, Geoffrey and I concentrated on keeping pace with the old man and on saving the remnants of our umbrella from the gusts. We seemed to be heading toward a small, ivy-covered building on a knoll just ahead. I tried to get a good look at the place but tripped over an exposed root. From then on I just concentrated on putting one foot in front of the other and listening to the sucking of water in my shoes.

After what seemed an eternity, our guide stopped in front of the mini-mausoleum. He rattled a large, corroded key in the lock, and grunted his satisfaction as the panel creaked inward. A single overhead bulb sprang to life, bathing the interior with its glare. The room glared back. It was positively bleak. Geoffrey and I followed Jasper through the entrance and looked around. There wasn't a stick of furniture. There wasn't a picture on the walls or a cross or anything. Except for two tiny ivy-clogged windows near the ceiling, the place looked like a crypt. One wall was fitted with a steel, arch-shaped door and some controls. That was all that broke the monotony of brick and stone.

"Should it be said one more time—people are just dying to come in here?" Weston asked, shedding his coat.

"They are for a fact," Thompson agreed wryly. He pointed to the crematory with a touch of pride. "That beauty puts out almost eighteen hundred degrees. Real efficient she is. Air and gas come in from all around—even from under the coffin when she's slid in."

Geoffrey pushed the disc covering the peep hole aside and peered through the opening.

"How long does it take to do its job?"

"No more'n two hours," Jasper bragged. "But then it takes five more for the brick lining to cool down."

Geoffrey stood staring for a long moment into the machine. He seemed lost in thought.

"You know, Jasper," he reflected, "you and I are privileged people. We are exposed to death in all of its starkness—minus the cosmetic touches that society has invented to soothe the feeble-souled. You watch as bodies are reduced to ashes. I inspect corpses long before they're decked out in topcoat and tails. Neither of us can avoid facing up to our own mortality, can we?"

Thompson nodded ever so slightly.

"You're right, Mr. Weston. The man's a fool who never thinks of his own death."

"And," my partner added, "the man's a fool who realizes the shortness of his life on earth but still does nothing about eternity. I hope you meant the words of that John Newton hymn you were singing back in the church."

"Every one of 'em," the caretaker assured him. "Been a Christian since just after the last Graham Crusade."

"Good for you," Geoffrey responded. "Good for you." He raised the handle with a clang and jerked the metal door wide open. "You say whole coffins are put in here. What about the nails?"

Jasper squeezed the water out of his hat before replying.

"Doesn't make any difference whether there's nails or whether there isn't. They burn up. All we ever get out after the furnace is fired is wedding rings and the like. Now your chrome steel is different too. It doesn't melt 'til six or seven hundred degrees hotter than our oven gets. The fire just turns it black, that's all."

While Geoffrey was talking with the caretaker, I began my investigation of the building entrance. Jasper had used that ancient key in the door for a very good reason. The modern dead-bolt lock that had secured the premises was missing—replaced by a gaping hole. The intruder had simply sawed a circle around it. The room was a cracker box. But then who would expect a break-in into a crematorium anyway! A foot below the lock I noticed the primitive alarm—an electrical contact that completed a circuit when the door was closed. Amazing that it had even been installed! More amazing that it had worked! By force of habit I took out my glass and focused on the device. It was then that I saw . . .

"Geoffrey, come over here and tell me what you make of this," I said, gesturing toward the spot.

Weston slammed the crematory closed and ambled over. He slipped his own magnifier out of his pocket and stooped to have a look.

"Notice the lines above and below the alarm contact," I directed. "They look very much like glue."

Geoffrey's eyes narrowed as he studied the marks. He used his pocket knife to scrape off a sample for a specimen envelope.

"That not only resembles glue," my colleague observed as he stood up. "It *is* glue—the gummy kind used on electrical tape. Without checking, I can tell you you'll find the same thing on the doorjamb. Our intruder attached two ends of a wire to the contacts so he could open the door without breaking the circuit."

"But," I pointed out, "the alarm *went off.* Do you think he botched the job?"

Weston returned the knife to his pocket with an air of satisfaction.

"No, I don't. If he had, he would have abandoned his scheme and run. He needed time for the crematory to work, and he couldn't know how long it would take for the clanging to arouse the neighborhood. It's almost certain that he entered undetected but yanked the wires out *as he was leaving.*"

"Then he didn't care if his act was discovered that night."

"Perhaps," Geoffrey concluded, "he wanted it to be."

Jasper, who had followed my partner over to the entrance, squeezed by us and ran his finger over the contact on the door post.

"You're right, Mr. Weston," he declared. "It's a mite sticky. What a relief! Thought I'd slept a while before hearing the alarm. Worried I was getting on in years."

Geoffrey slapped the old man on the back.

"The way you had us puffing to keep up, Thompson, I'd say we're the ones in danger of doddering. Would you like to help us go over the floor for clues?"

Jasper brightened noticeably.

"Indeed I would. Never done any detective work before. It'll be something to write the grandchildren about."

"Good. We'll divide the room into thirds. You take the area by the door." He handed the gentleman a plastic envelope. "If you find anything, put it in here."

The three of us began going over the floor inch by inch. Geoffrey crisscrossed his area, casting about like some bloodhound after a scent. I worked side to side with the precision of a typewriter—examining parallel rows. Weston called it my "hunt and peek system." Jasper crawled around in his shirt sleeves with that soggy hat dangling out of his hip pocket. His broad grin was the final touch which could have placed him among the quaint characters painted by the American artist, Norman Rockwell.

After a painstaking half-hour my specimen pouch was still empty. Glancing in my partner's direction, I could see that he wasn't faring any better. Jasper would at least have some sawdust samples. I knew Geoff had put him by the door for that very reason. But when I looked up to check, I got a real surprise.

"Where on earth," I asked, "did that cat come from?"

The caretaker was sitting next to the wall with a scrawny half-grown kitten in his lap. The animal might have once been presentable. But now—dirty, wet, and shivering—it was a most pitiful creature.

"There are a lot of them around here," Jasper explained softly while stroking its matted fur. "People drop them off and congratulate themselves for not drowning the poor things. Most starve or are put to sleep. I help the few I can."

Geoffrey shook his head sympathetically.

"Sometimes," he confessed, "I find myself angry with mankind. How we pervert the dominion over nature that God has given us! Dominion— we all want that. But we lack the love and compassion that distinguish sovereignty from tyranny."

"Would you take him?" Thompson invited. "I can't care for any more cats right now."

I have seldom seen Geoffrey at a loss for words. But he was now. He didn't want a pet and I knew it. But he could hardly harangue for compassion in one breath and in the next breath refuse to show it. Thompson's simple directness had him in a box. Geoff looked at me questioningly. I nodded ascent and the decision was made. We had another boarder at Number 31, Baker Street. I abandoned my fruitless search of the floor and went over to greet the latest addition to the firm. The kitten struggled briefly as Jasper handed him to me, but finally settled in my arms and began to purr.

"The little dickens likes me," I remarked. "He's probably never been shown much affection."

Geoffrey now came over himself and stroked the kitten under the chin. Resigned to having a cat, he clearly intended to enjoy it.

"He does for a fact, old boy. What shall we call him? Wilberforce? No, that doesn't have the right ring to it. How about Blackstone?"

"For a white cat?" I protested.

"You have a point. Is Gladstone any better?"

"Gladstone . . . " I savored the name. The kitten continued to purr. "That doesn't sound half bad. He's glad all right. And I guess the late prime minister won't mind."

"Then Gladstone it is," Weston concluded. "An unusual stone to bring home from a cemetery, wouldn't you say?"

I groaned and shook my head.

"I might have known you'd discover a pun in this someplace. Let's get the creature back to Baker Street before we're all stone cold."

Weston glanced back at the area he'd been searching.

"Just a moment, old boy, and we can be on our way. But first I want a quick look at that corner we missed."

As I waited impatiently, Geoffrey made one last pass over the floor and satisfied himself that we had overlooked nothing. While he did so, Jasper gave me his specimen bag crammed with soggy sawdust. And the two of us bundled up again in preparation for re-entering the elements. Thompson had a decided advantage over me since he'd worn a slicker. I had not expected rain that morning and my old wool greatcoat offered almost no protection. Nevertheless, I tucked Gladstone inside and he seemed content.

"Remember," Thompson reminded me, "to give him his injections as soon as possible." With his shrill voice he sounded like a two-hundred-pound mother hen. I nodded solemnly.

"Rest assured that he'll have the best of care. His biggest problem," I chuckled, "is going to be finding an empty ledge to perch on. Our quarters—"

"That does it, John," Geoffrey interrupted. He retrieved his coat and began buttoning up. "Thank you for your assistance, Mr. Thompson. Let me know if we can ever be of help to you."

My partner walked briskly through the open door and held the umbrella over our heads as Jasper locked up.

The wind howled plaintively as it swirled among the monuments. But the downpour didn't seem quite as fierce as before. Actually I suppose I was a trifle numb. The return didn't seem half the ordeal that the outward trek had been. In an amazingly short time I could make out the parking lights of our station wagon in the distance. Within minutes, Geoff had slid behind the wheel and was turning the key in the ignition. I held my breath—hoping for dry wires. On the third try the engine cranked rapidly, sputtered and roared to life. We waved good-bye to the caretaker and backed out onto Old Brompton Road.

* * * * *

I have seldom enjoyed a bath as much as I did that afternoon. Piping hot water slowly dissolved the grit and chill of the graveyard and restored me to good spirits. After dressing, shaving, and combing my hair I actually felt like facing the world again. Geoffrey hadn't showered, but a change of clothing had evidently done wonders for him also. As I neared the kitchen I could hear him whistling a theme from Haydn's "Creation" and clanking pans together. The teapot was also whistling, and the aroma of clam chowder filled the air. Geoffrey looked up as I entered.

"You took long enough, John! I was beginning to think you'd caught your toe in the drain."

I ignored his comment and poured myself a cup of tea.

"What," I asked between sips, "is on the agenda for tonight? It's starting to sleet outside, and I don't fancy going on another safari."

"You shant," my colleague assured me as he dipped a ladle into the steaming soup. "If we need any more evidence, we'll send out for it. I may make a brief jaunt myself later on."

"And the cat?"

"He's clean, fluffy, and stuffed to the whiskers with milk and sardines. You'll find him in a box by the fireplace."

I elected, however, to lift the lid from a second pot on the stove.

"Ah, white fish with asparagus and cheese! What's on the back burner?"

"Green peas and mint," Weston replied. "If you'll grab a couple of dishes out of the sink and clean them off, we can get started."

As I washed, Geoffrey poured the soup and laid out the silverware. "Lord Jesus, we thank you for this food," began my partner after sitting up to the table. "And thanks for the weather too! Amen."

As he finished praying I felt the sudden urge to comment on his "love" for rain but choked on the words. Instead I was reminded of the proverb which says: "A man of understanding keeps silence." So the first few moments were spent in silence—savoring every bite and taking the edge off my hunger. But after a second cup of tea, my thoughts started to wander from the meal to the mystery before us. I speared a piece of fish with my fork; then hesitated before lifting it to my mouth.

"Who was that who rang while I was dressing?" I inquired. "The Inspector?"

"A shrewd guess," Weston noted approvingly. He swallowed before continuing. "Twigg had the results of the spectrographic test for us."

"And?"

"And," my partner admitted, "it showed the metal in the joint to be identical with that used in James Chester's bone. I took the liberty of calling Mrs. Chester after that to see if she could have those business records for us a bit ahead of schedule. I'm beginning to think time may be important in this case. Incidentally, she told me that her husband wears a wedding band."

"So?"

Weston leaned back and drank his fill of tea. He was clearly irritated that I didn't appreciate the tidbit.

"John, stop being dense. There are only two possibilities in this affair. Chester is either alive or he's dead. If he is alive and has merely perpetrated a hoax, then his actions must follow a logical pattern. Will you agree to that?"

"Most assuredly," I responded, "but what has that got to do with—"

"It has everything to do with the ring. If Chester wanted the world to assume him dead, he had to be certain that chrome steel would not melt in the crematory. Otherwise there would be no evidence left behind that could be traced to him. If he knew that, he must have also known that his ring wouldn't melt. But he didn't plant it with the joint!"

"Perhaps," I ventured, "he couldn't bear to part with it."

Weston gestured with his fork.

"I can't accept that. A man who abandons his wife—perhaps for another woman—isn't going to be sentimental. What's more, if he has an ounce of intelligence, he's not going to show up at work the next day to grade some silly papers."

"Then you think . . ."

"I'm absolutely certain," Geoffrey declared grimly. "James Chester was brutally murdered. The killer didn't know about the man's operation, so he assumed all the evidence would be destroyed in the flames. He removed the ring on the off-chance that it might not melt."

I paused to finish the last of the asparagus on my plate. The way Weston explained it everything seemed so simple, except . . .

"If Chester is dead," I pointed out, "then we're still left with some inexplainable day-after 'resurrection.' Wouldn't that argue against your theory?"

My partner nodded soberly.

"It would, indeed. I haven't quite got a grip on what that 'resurrection' was, but I will."

He stood up, stretched, and ceremoniously wiped his mouth on a napkin.

"I don't know about you," he declared, "but I'm going into the living room where there's space to pace. We have enough information now so that the answer should be obvious. And I won't rest tonight until I have an explanation for Chester's encore appearance."

The two of us cleared the table and stacked the dishes neatly in the sink. We followed the normal routine—salt onto the counter, pots into the ice-box, napkins into the hamper. Then we escaped to the living room.

I set up my microscope on a table in the corner and began sifting through the several envelopes we had accumulated, hoping to find some possible evidence. The hair in Chester's office proved to be non-human. The doctor must have allowed his monkey into the room. The crematorium sawdust was mixed with paint flakes that might prove embarrassing to the murderer if any had lodged in his trouser cuffs. While I worked, Geoffrey paced back and forth, brooded and muttered to himself. Once when I looked up I saw him reading the New Testament. For nearly an hour he traced and retraced his steps—pausing only to stroke his goatee or to fish peanuts out of a newly replenished dish on the mantle. Gladstone sat toasting himself by the fire and watching my colleague's every move. The spectacle was taking more than its fair share of my attention too.

"Perhaps it would help," I suggested at last, "if you talked about it."

Weston stopped to pull a journal down from the bookcase.

"It might at that," he admitted. "John, I believe the best way to detect a counterfeit is to examine the genuine—whether a person is testing ten-pound notes, Shakespearian sonnets, or perported resurrections. And the more I look at the genuine article, the learier I am of Chester's miraculous return. Lord Chillingham wrote a monograph on witness credibility that about sums up my own thinking. He examined the gospel account of Christ's resurrection and concluded . . . But it might be simpler to just read you a snatch of it." Geoffrey leafed through the magazine until he found the page he wanted. "Ah, here it is. Now as I read, keep in mind the witnesses' testimony to Chester's after-death appearance. Notice the difference." My partner cleared the cobwebs from his throat and started in halfway down the page:

> An APPARENT disparity between witnesses' statements may be a strong proof FOR witness reliability. Differing vantage points, a continually changing scene of action, and each person's unique estimate of what matters usually combine to produce variation in testimony. Such variation does not indicate error if differences can be logically explained. In fact, it is something to be desired. Identical accounts are danger signals warning of collusion between witnesses. Healthy, rational disparity, on the other hand, is the hallmark of honesty. The Bible accounts of the resurrection contain just such a hallmark.
>
> In the book of John, for example, Mary Magdalene describes her encounter with Jesus as though she and He were alone. In effect she tells John: "He appeared to ME!" She saw Jesus alive, and that was what registered. John doesn't mention that several other women were present because Mary didn't fill in that detail. Other wit-

> nesses in other gospels do. In the same way a straggler who is unable to squeeze into the empty tomb only tells Mark about the single angel visible through the doorway. One of the other women—who is able to get inside—sees two shining heavenly messengers and reports the complete picture to Luke. The resurrection of Christ and the resultant empty tomb thus must be accepted as valid historical events. Each witness to the events tells a slightly different story. But the testimonies complement rather than contradict one another.

Geoffrey closed the journal and returned it to the shelf before continuing.

"Lord Chillingham goes on to describe the solid physical evidence that proves Jesus' disciples were not deceived. Jesus was not merely seen. He was heard and touched. He ate food provided by the witnesses. He allowed them to stick their fingers into His scars and check for gimmicks. Their every sense (except possibly the sense of taste) told them that Jesus was *alive*—resurrected from the dead. Now how does all that compare with Chester's paper grading?"

"Well," I ventured, "Hill, Meyer and company all tell pretty much the same story. There's not much variation."

"Not much?" my colleague spat out in disgust. "John, there isn't *any* except for Hill's very uncertain remarks about the smoke! Chester doesn't get up and pour himself a cup of hot chocolate. He doesn't sneeze. He doesn't wave. For twenty solid minutes he doesn't do anything but puff and grade, puff and grade. And at the end of that time the cigar is still as long as it was at the beginning! The widow's cruse I will believe. But the teacher's cigar, never!"

"Perhaps," I suggested, "one of the witnesses was mistaken about the length. Or it may have gone out."

Geoffrey began pacing again.

"I've thought of that," he confessed. "But neither alternative makes sense. Singleton, Johnson, Meyer, and Hill all say they saw a smoke-filled room with an open window. If the cigar kept going out, the room would have cleared of smoke. If it didn't go out, it would have been over an inch shorter by the time Miss Meyer passed by—a very recognizable change. It's amazing also that Mr. Hill saw a just-lighted cigar *and* a smoke-filled room. Unless Chester had only recently finished another smoke, I wouldn't expect that. And, as you know, we only have the ashes from a single cigar."

"Which," I pointed out, "must, therefore, have been a long rather than a medium."

Geoffrey paused to grab another handful of peanuts.

"No, it wasn't. For one thing there isn't enough ash. For another, I found a couple of Chester's cigars in the desk. They are mediums—exactly four and three-quarters inches long. The three-quarters of an inch would have been in his mouth. Therefore, my friend, we are stuck with four witnesses speaking identical nonsense. And we haven't a shred of *physical* evidence that James Chester was in the room."

"How can you say that," I questioned, "when you yourself have just talked about an ash?"

"Oh, that." Weston waved his arm in the air in dismissal. "That is simply an undated remnant. Judging from the amount of droppings in the trash basket, I would say Chester was strongly addicted to his vice. But we have the remains of only one cigar for *two* days of smoking. Do you think it more logical that he smoked that cylinder the day before or the day after he was apparently murdered?"

I nodded thoughtfully.

"When you put it that way, there isn't much of a choice, is there?"

"No, there isn't," my partner agreed. "And when you add to that that three of the four witnesses are sure they smelled no smoke as they stood in front of the open window on a *calm* day, it is nearly certain that Chester wasn't puffing a physical cigar."

"Why then did Hill think he smelled smoke?"

Geoffrey smiled and bent down to pet Gladstone—who yawned and basked in the attention.

"Once," he replied, "I bought a grape soda from a vending machine. But the machine malfunctioned and I got Coca Cola in my cup. The lighting was too dim for me to notice the switch. I tell you that was the strangest tasting concoction I've ever drunk! My mind said grape. My tongue said Coke. And the stuff ended up with a flavor somewhere in between. In the same way Stephen Hill expected to smell smoke, so he did. And look at Miss Meyer's rationalizing. If I hadn't cut her off, she would have had the whole room remembering an odor they never smelled and throwing flowers at Chester for his good taste in tobacco! The mind may twist truth to preserve its sense of being logical."

"You've pretty well ruled out," I conceded, "that James Chester was physically present in the office. Solid, living men don't smoke odorless, self-renewing cigars. So I'll accept your theory that the man was murdered the night before. But what options does that leave us with? No actor could have done an impersonation. Even the best of staging wouldn't have produced the eerie effects you've just described. Are we back to the demonic?"

"Possibly," my partner concluded as he stood up and resumed his trek. "I did find a book on extra-sensory perception in the professor's library. He may have dabbled in the occult—all in the name of science, of course. But I'm not totally convinced that we have anything paranormal here. If Satan really wanted to imitate Chester—for whatever reason—he could have orchestrated a much more effective production. Then there's the matter of the missing dust . . . No, John, I'm more inclined toward the illusion or delusion theory."

"By which you mean?"

"We know that the witnesses didn't kill the professor and then invent a story about seeing him. If that had happened, Miss Meyer wouldn't have passed the polygraph test. But they might have been hypnotized by the murderer and instructed to see what they think they saw. A good hypnotist—perhaps one of Chester's colleagues—could have made them forget the hypnotic sessions as well as rendering them immune to future tampering. We already know that Hill and Singleton underwent counseling—which makes the theory somewhat attractive. And it would explain both the identical stories and the odorless smoke. The four might not have smelled anything unless specifically ordered to do so.

"There's also a possibility that the murderer may have used some sort of projection device to create the impression that Chester was in his office. Notice that all the witnesses viewed the man from nearly identical locations. But there are technical problems with that idea. Intense outdoor light eliminates the chance that a rear projection screen was placed across the entire window. Colors would have washed out and the hoax would have been obvious. A screen well inside the room would have appeared extremely flat and could not have been made to blend with the natural objects in the room. Three-dimensional projections would—by their very nature—have been off in color. And a simple Disneyland-style robot equipped with a rear projection screen as a face might have given a convincing performance, but it still would not account for the smoke."

I held one of the buttons Geoffrey had found up to the light. It was mother-of-pearl—probably from a woman's blouse. And it almost certainly had nothing to do with the case.

"Well," I sympathized, "you do seem to be rather at an impasse. But isn't it enough just to know that the professor was murdered? Surely we can investigate on that premise until we find someone with a motive. By that time new developments may cause the person's methods to become obvious."

"You're right, of course," Weston grudgingly admitted. "But it's dreadfullly galling to be so close to solving the puzzle and to know you're trying to force a key piece in upside down! I feel as inadequate as Jacob must have felt during his wrestling match."

"But in this case you don't have to fight on until morning," I reminded him. "Why not go have your session with Ruth Chester and then stop by the racquet club for a couple of sets of tennis. Even the indoor courts should have openings on a night like this. Take your mind off the problem. Tomorrow everything may fall into place."

Geoffrey frowned as he considered my suggestion—then forced himself to relax. I could almost see the tension drain from his face, but I knew the adrenalin was still pumping. Like someone speeding for hours on a motorway and then suddenly turning off onto a country lane, he needed time to adjust to the change in pace. Without a word he walked over to the closet and dug his tennis equipment out from the bottom of the pile.

"I think I'll take that suggestion, John. Where's my trench coat? Oh, here it is. Should anyone ring, tell him I may be late. If I run across any leads, I shall follow them up."

With racquet in one hand, balls in the other, and shoes slung over his shoulder, Weston strode across the room and out into the night. I went back to analyzing evidence.

Within the hour, two pages of notes summarized my findings. Every speck of dust, dirt and ash had been returned to its envelope, and I didn't know a whole lot more than I had when I started. So I took my own advice and retreated to an overstuffed easy chair for some leisurely Bible study. Not unnaturally I found myself thumbing through the Gospels and comparing the writers' treatments of the resurrection. There were far more variations than Geoffrey had mentioned. But Lord Chillingham's premise held firm. I could almost see the disciples looking on from various angles. Some even skipped events in order to hurry and describe their personal encounter with the Lord. None copied the others. And none strayed from the truth. The accounts intermeshed as perfectly as the gears of a fine watch.

At nine o'clock I switched on the telly and tuned in to the ITV channel where I was urged to "Hava-cup-a Typhoo Tea." When I didn't, the announcer faded off the screen in disgust—making way for a Muppet rerun. Not very intellectual fare perhaps, but I enjoyed it. Shortly after that I retired for the evening. Geoffrey still had not returned.

CHAPTER 4
The Man Machine

Before dawn, I was rudely awakened by the jangle of our telephone. I groaned and rolled over. But it wouldn't stop. So I grabbed a robe from the nightstand and groped my way to the living room. Switching on the light, I opened one eye just enough to make out the receiver and pick it up.

"Hallo."

My partner's voice resounded metalically in the earpiece.

"Well, John, good to see you up and about. The game's afoot. And we can't sleep through the whole day, can we?"

"Weston," I managed groggily, "it's positively indecent of you to be cheerful at this hour. What time is it, anyway? And why the call?"

"It's fifty-nine minutes to six, mate. And we have a busy schedule for the morning. If you can get here within the next half hour or so, we'll be able to reach Faversham before businesses open."

"That's wonderful," I declared in a tone that implied it wasn't. "Why on earth would anyone want to go there?"

Geoffrey chuckled. "We can talk about that on

the way. But right now time is of the essence. Take the Bakerloo line to the Elephant and Castle station. I'm two blocks north—just off of Newington Causeway. The address is 317 Gaunt."

A long, satisfying yawn escaped my mouth.

"Hold on a moment while I dig up a pencil." Some rummaging produced a stub and the back of an envelope. "What's that number again?"

"Three seventeen Gaunt. It's a large, white building."

"Barring accidents," I promised, "you'll see me shortly. Will you be waiting outside?"

"Not if I can help it. There are three inches of snow on the ground. But my project here should be just about finished by the time you arrive. Cheerio."

The line went dead. Now fully awake, I made a brief stop in the kitchen to pop a muffin into the toaster before retracing my steps to the bedroom. By the time I returned, fully dressed, the muffin was piping hot and ready for the jelly. I grabbed it on the run, slipped into a coat, and walked out the front door.

Baker Street's wide sidewalk sparkled under the street lamps. And the lights of the city—reflected back from low clouds—softly accented a wall-to-wall blanket of white. What had only a few hours before been a foreboding scene was transformed into a fairyland. As I buttoned my coat against the chill I marvelled at the crisp air and the holiday appearance of the brownstones across the way—now sporting snowy bonnets marred only by an occasional chimney.

I walked briskly up the street toward Marylebone. The city was still fast asleep, and the silence was broken only by the crunching under my feet. Every now and then a motorcar drove gingerly by—trying to avoid skids. Otherwise, nothing stirred. The underground station lay three blocks away but seemed much closer. It was with some regret that I neared the entrance.

The stairway into the tube led past the usual rogues' gallery of advertising posters. I purchased my ticket at a booth, inserted it into the turnstyle, and walked out onto the platform. A snack shoppe was just opening up, but there wasn't time to make a visit. Within two minutes an ultra-modern, large-windowed train slowed to a stop a few feet away. It was on the Bakerloo line and headed downtown. A door slid open and I stepped inside.

* * * * *

The building looked very much as Geoffrey had described it. It was certainly big enough and completely white. But my colleague had neglected to mention the large aluminum letters spread across the front. I had arrived at "The South London Applied Physics Laboratory." Judging from the snow on our Mercedes parked in the drive, Geoffrey had been there the better part of the night.

As I neared the motorcar, my friend came bounding down the laboratory steps. At the rate he was traveling, it was amazing he didn't fall and break his neck. He waved me toward the passenger side.

"John, there's not a moment to waste. Scrape

the windows and let's take to the road. Some lives may depend upon our swift action."

I set to work as Weston coaxed the engine to life. Soon we pulled cautiously out onto the street and picked up speed. Geoffrey maneuvered with the sure hand of a professional—maintaining control but pushing the station wagon to its safe limits. We wove in and out through the early-morning traffic and finally mounted a ramp to the comparatively easy driving of a motorway. It was only then that I ventured to speak.

"Now that we can relax a mite, will you please bring me up-to-date on what's happening? I'm dying of curiosity."

Weston didn't take his eyes off the road, but he gestured with his head toward the shadowy rear seat. His voice was serious.

"If you'll look at the folder back there, you'll get part of the picture. We seem to be swimming in suspects."

"And that," I asked archly, "is what opened the door to a research facility in the dead of night and induced you to while away your hours there?"

"Hardly," my partner admitted. He turned on the heater and held his free hand over a defrosting vent for an interminable period before continuing. "Do you remember Sterling Mallory—the chap we helped out in the Bradford jewel case? Well, he's on the board of South London Applied Physics, and he pulled some strings. Actually, you're the one responsible for my wanting to use the facility."

"I—"

"Certainly. You said something last night—without intending to—that set me to thinking. 'New developments' was the expression you used. And I've been experimenting with some."

"Would you," I commented dryly, "care to be more specific?"

Geoffrey smiled his most tormenting smile. He has a habit at times of being deliberately vague. When he answered it was with a touch of banter.

"Not really. If everything goes well, you'll see for yourself in a few hours. I love surprises, don't you? By the way, did you know that James Chester was interested in cryogenics?"

"What," I asked in exasperation, "does that have to do with anything?"

"Oh nothing . . . " My partner glanced casually at the glow on the horizon. " . . . except that we are en route to visit with a Mr. Bertram Seawell, president of Consolidated Cryogenics. James Chester's library contains an autographed book by the fellow. And the professor's financial records show he was receiving a stipend from the company. That strikes me as highly peculiar! And I've learned to be wary of oddities. As often as not they are clues in disguise."

I was incredulous.

"Do you mean that we're sitting here watching the sunrise all because of some business connection of Chester's? Couldn't we have waited for a more convenient time to look into the matter?"

Weston sighed. For just an instant his lack of sleep showed.

"Perhaps, John. Perhaps not. But Mr. Seawell

may be a suspect or a potential victim. In either case he needs to be spoken with quickly. I don't want another murder on our hands."

We drove on in silence. I knew Geoffrey was thinking back a year to Arthur Heath's tragic death in the Dorking affair. He still felt that he might have kept the man alive, although I don't know how. And he was going to be liberal with his warnings in this new case. The powerful engine in the Mercedes droned on and consumed the kilometers. Since it was still too dark to read the folder, I leaned back, relaxed, and closed my eyes.

* * * * *

When my partner shook me awake, the sun was up and so were we—on a hill. The station wagon came to a halt in front of a sprawling, low-slung building that resembled a mansion suffering from indecision. It had enough wings to fly.

"So this," I managed between yawns, "is Consolidated Cryogenics. It looks more like a rest home."

"As a matter of fact," Geoffrey corrected, "it is neither. I called Seawell's wife last night and set up a seven o'clock appointment at his home. Bertram seems to be rather well off, wouldn't you say?"

"Either that," I agreed, "or he found a dandy tax sale. What say we stroll on in and get acquainted."

The two of us were met at the door by a lanky fellow dressed for a ball and starched to the toes. Clyde, the butler, escorted us to the master's study where we sat in plush chairs and watched our shoes disappear into the nap of the carpet. Bertram Seawell had a movie mogul's flair for opulence! While Clyde went to fetch our host, I could see Geoffrey's hawkish gaze survey in turn every detail of the room—from the knife collection hung on the walls, to the suit of armor in the corner, to the solid mahogany woodwork.

A balding, middle-aged gentleman made a grand entrance and walked over to us with hand outstretched. Neither the paunch nor his slightly walleyed stare detracted from his air of authority. He spoke with a resonant, self-assured voice.

"It's good to meet both of you. Sally told me I was in for a rare treat this morning and . . . well, I agree. I've followed your activities with a good deal of interest, Mr. Weston—between trips out of the country, that is. Have a seat and state your business."

My partner dropped Seawell's pumping hand and we complied. Bertram, however, maintained a psychological advantage by continuing to stand. He was every inch a salesman.

"The newspapers," Geoffrey acknowledged modestly, "tend to exaggerate when they write about me. But I trust that our visit may be to some degree productive. Rest assured that we won't take too much of your time. We're here investigating a murder, the murder of James Chester, and—"

"Jim, dead!" The words gushed out of our host's mouth mixed with horror and disbelief. His face flushed to almost the color of his vest. The man appeared stunned. But then he visibly caught hold of himself and continued with a forced levelness. "You're certain?"

"Yes, quite," Weston assured him. "And we came across your name among the victim's possessions. Do you know of anyone who might have had a motive for killing him?"

Still shaken, Bertram nervously patted his shirt pocket in the manner of the habitual smoker. But the pocket was empty.

"Frankly I don't," he decided at length, "unless it might be one of the crazies he's been helping."

"By that you mean?"

"I don't know their names. But he worked with some of the students."

Geoffrey's features were as hard as flint. He studied the man with a critical eye.

"And what conceivable connection," he demanded, "could Chester have had with Consolidated Cryogenics?"

In answer Seawell picked a silver whistle off the desk and blew a shrill blast on it. He looked for all the world like some pompous and portly ring master announcing the next act.

"In just a moment, Mr. Weston, you will see what Jim did for us." He smiled disarmingly. "It was entirely within his area of professional competence, I assure you."

Consolidated's president gazed toward the hall expectantly, and we found ourselves doing likewise. I fully imagined that Clyde would come in bearing a ledger on a gold platter. Bertram whistled again.

"He should be here any time now. It's a goodly distance from the playroom. Oh, there you are! Come to papa."

A large chimpanzee wearing a red and white jumper romped through the door and sprang into Seawell's arms. The animal looked for all the world like a child craving affection. And "papa" staggered under the sudden weight.

"This," our host managed above the creature's raucous cries, "is Chi Chi. Chester trained her for us."

"You can't mean," I stammered—my mouth wanting to hang open, "that a psychologist specialized in producing pet monkeys!"

"Hardly," my partner assured me. He then addressed Seawell. "I take it that Consolidated is in some way employing chimps in its research. Would you care to tell us for what purpose they are used and how your friend fits into the picture?"

"Certainly." Bertram disentangled himself from the animal's arms and put it down. His words assumed a pedantic tone. "To be perfectly blunt about it, we've been putting them into suspended animation. You are aware, of course, that chimpanzees have excellent memories. Jim's job was to condition each chimp before freezing so that it had a large response vocabulary. After resuscitation, he evaluated each animal to check for memory loss or emotional instability. So far we've been able to freeze the creatures for up to six months with minimal ill effects. Chi Chi here was asleep for four. As you can see, she's perfectly normal."

"Amazing!" I enthused. "But what's the good of it all?"

Bertram clasped what would have been the lapels of his vest if vests had lapels. He obviously enjoyed talking about his work.

"A good question, sir. I would not be investing a fortune in these experiments if they weren't practical. And I frankly believe that what we're doing surpasses in importance even Francis Crick's breaking of the DNA code. Think of the possibilities once we've perfected the technique for use on humans! For one thing, it opens up the stars for colonization by man. Astronauts will be able to sleep a thousand years in transit. And consider the injured or terminally ill. They can be frozen until medicine advances to the point of restoring them to health. Ultimately, every dying person on the globe will be treated cryogenically and stored for the day when science learns to reverse the aging process." His voice swelled with pride. "Gentlemen, we are literally standing at the threshhold of immortality!"

Weston eyed the tycoon coolly.

"I think I prefer, Seawell, the immortality I've already got."

Bertram looked puzzled. He had evidently expected us to share his exuberance.

"I don't understand what you're—"

"I'm talking," Geoffrey filled in, "about conversion, heaven, and a new, *indestructible* body."

Our host slapped his forehead in consternation.

"Oh, how stupid of me! Of course. You're one of those evangelical chaps that make life so unpleasant. And a man of your stature! I wouldn't have believed it. Pie in the sky and all that!"

"I would rather have pie in the sky," Weston countered with a tinge of sarcasm, "than to content myself with crumbs on the ground as you are doing. If you really want to live forever, put your faith where it will do some good."

"Faith!" Bertram laughed. "I'm a self-made man, Mr. Weston. I have faith in what I see and do—not in some 'way out there' experience. And I cannot accept the idea of heaven. Man is an electro-chemical machine. No more, no less! When the current stops and the compounds become unstable, man no longer exists."

Geoffrey shook his head in pity and disappointment before answering.

"I see that you admire more in Crick than his DNA achievements. You seem to have swallowed his philosophy. But be careful. I, for one, find it difficult to accept the speculations of machines. And you—viewing yourself as a machine—will one day have to abandon faith in even yourself. Thoughts may be malfunctions, and faith is—after all—a *human* trait."

"You can bandy words around," our host responded with annoyance, "but when you are dust and I'm still walking around and breathing fresh air, all of your arguments will be so much garbage."

" 'When . . .' " Weston savored the word. " 'When . . . I'm still walking around.' You sound as though you definitely have *faith* in your materialistic salvation. You have almost the same atheistic confidence that communists show in the—to them—inevitable flow of history. But it's an ignorant faith, Seawell. Can't you see? Voltaire for once was right when he said that this isn't the best of all possible worlds. It's not. Rebellion against God has turned it into very much of a mixed bag. You don't even know if you will live long enough to get frozen! One bullet in the brain and your dreams of 'glory' are crushed. And if you do manage to be 'immortalized' in ice, who operates the controls for the next thousand years? What prevents power failures? How do you know you won't be terminated by an earthquake, a flood, nuclear holocaust, or any of a dozen other disasters? You don't. You can't. You claim confidence in yourself, but your real confidence lies in some anonymous future keepers and in the turn of the wheel."

Bertram sat down on the edge of the desk and considered for a moment. His lips were pressed so hard together that they showed traces of white. My partner had hit a nerve. Finally our host nodded grudging assent.

"You're right, of course, Weston. My longevity is rather provisional, isn't it? What do you think the probabilities are? Ten percent? Twenty? That's not overly comforting. But it's still better than zero. And by careful choice of location, backup equipment and future personnel, I may be able to improve my chances. Thank you for pointing out the weaknesses in my plan."

I stared at the man in utter disbelief. He seemed rational enough, but . . .

"How can you," I shuddered, "speak that way about your own life! You're not talking about some abstract experiment, man. You're playing the odds with your own destiny!"

"And you," Seawell retorted heatedly, "are sitting around like lemmings—doing nothing. Blandly awaiting your own extinction. Sedated to the point of complacency by the opium of religion. I'm a fighter. And I'll fight for life even beyond my last breath!"

Geoffrey stood up and solemnly addressed the man. His every word fell with the methodical force of a blacksmith's hammer.

"Three cheers for good old British self-sufficiency! You are the master of your fate, the captain of your electro-chemical life. But that pose—and that's all it is—is a mask for something not quite so imposing. I think you're struggling from a sense of panic. Jesus' disciples died willingly as the price for telling others that Christ *really arose.* They suffered through shipwreck, beatings and stonings to declare that Jesus gives life to those who repent and trust in Him. That, my friend, is strength based upon reality. But your 'fight' is a clinging to every heartbeat with the white knuckles of desperation. 'Live,' you command yourself. 'Live long enough to be successfully frozen.' You turn every breath into the hell of uncertainty. Will there be another? Or will your tobacco-clogged lungs give up the ghost? You fight for life and destroy its beauty. You struggle against destruction and destroy your very humanity in the process. Mister machine, if you're only a machine, you don't deserve to live forever! And if you're more, then your premise is wrong.

"Frankly, Bertram, you worry me. Your concept of people is dangerously low. And you have such a strong instinct for survival! Would you eliminate an electro-chemical machine, I wonder, that stood in the way of your reaching your goal? What are the probabilities, mate, that you murdered James Chester?"

For the second time in the conversation our host seemed stunned. He stared at us blankly for just an instant. Then I could see his jaw set as anger took over. His fist slammed down on the desk, sending the whistle slithering across the room.

"Get out of my house," he commanded icily. "I never want to see you two rogues again."

"If you wish," Weston replied with firmness. "But there is one thing further that you should know. If you're not the murderer, you may be his next victim. I should take some precautions if I were you."

"Out!" Seawell shouted—now livid with rage. "Get out or I'll have you thrown out!"

Without saying another word, my partner and I walked out the door.

* * * * *

As we drove down the motorway once again I reached toward the back seat and picked up the folder. There would be time enough during our return to the city to catch up on my homework.

"An excitable fellow, isn't he?" I thought aloud. "I wonder if he's capable of killing."

Geoffrey steered the Mercedes into the right lane and passed a pickup.

"I don't know," he mused. "Seawell certainly

is arrogant. And he's used to bending people to his way of thinking. Add that to a violent temper, and there isn't much I'd put past him. But we don't know that Chester ever opposed him. And Bertram really seemed upset when he heard about his friend's death." Weston switched on the radio and dialed until he found soft instrumental music. "Seawell may or may not be the murderer."

I began working my way through the folder. Chester had evidently written out a personality profile on each of his six clients. As I turned the pages scanning the contents, I let out a low whistle. What a motley crew they were! We already had sampled George Singleton's temper. But the tantrum he had thrown for us only rated a one point nine on the Richter scale compared to the rage which had once sent his own father to the hospital! Stephen Hill was just as much a character. He'd left prep school before graduation to wander for several years as a hippy. But some twenty months ago the luster had worn off. A diploma came easily, and he went on to college—carrying claustrophobia along as a memento of his vagabond period. June Albey had also experienced mental shipwreck as a dropout. LSD flashbacks tormented her, and she was haunted by the memory of an aborted daughter. Jason Phelp's life had been routine enough. But he was nagged by a vague, faceless fear. Things had gotten so bad that he had to force himself to even go outside his apartment. Cathy Hopkins stepped on every crack in the sidewalk—no doubt from some deep-seated desire to "break her mother's back." She touched every picket in the fences she walked beside. And she painted with extraordinary attention to detail. Jackson Smyth vascilated between feverish activity and periods of depression. Even mood-changing drugs administered by one of Chester's doctor friends had not been of much help. In short, James Chester had treated every mental illness this side of catatonia! And we were faced with a wild assortment of suspects.

I put down the papers and shifted my attention to the scenery. By now the road had turned to slush. Nearby maples and pines were shedding their icicles. And the sky was clearing. The trip back to London was uneventful. We arrived in time for a late breakfast at the Simple Simon.

CHAPTER 5

The Unmasking

"I must be mad to let you talk me into these things," Twigg complained. "You'd think a body had nothing better to do than stand in the snow and watch steam come out of his mouth!"

We were waiting in front of the "temporary" almost directly opposite the window to Chester's office. And both the Inspector and I knew that Weston was about to stage one of his theatrical demonstrations. Geoffrey had only shortly before carried a mysterious box into the building—one that we had picked up at Mallory's laboratory on Gaunt. And my partner had the look of an actor psyched up and ready to step onto center stage. I stomped my feet in a vain attempt to chase away the numbness.

"Geoff, I have to agree with the Inspector. If those patients of Chester's don't start arriving soon, I'm going inside to heat up some of the professor's chocolate. Much more of this and you'll go to gaol for causing our death of pneumonia."

Weston surveyed the sidewalk in both directions and nodded his head in agreement.

"That would prove rather embarrassing,

wouldn't it? But I think that ball of fur approaching may be one of the young ladies. Pull up a snow drift and stay awhile. This should be interesting."

"I'm sure your own flaky drift," Twigg commented wryly, "will be enough of a 'snow job' for us all. What part do you want me to play in these proceedings?"

"Since we don't have an opening for a comedian," my partner replied, "why don't you keep the suspects busy so I can speak with them one at a time?"

Twigg would have responded, but fortunately the young lady called out, asking if we were the police. It was back to business for us all! We were approached by a striking brunette in an Eskimo coat and mittens. Her cheeks rosey from the cold wind, she seemed the picture of health and vitality. When within arms' reach she stuck out her hand to me.

"Hello, I'm June Albey. You wanted to ask me some questions?"

"Actually," I corrected, "it's Geoffrey there that will do the talking. I'm John Taylor and that's Inspector Twigg."

She looked brightly at the three of us. Her accent, when she spoke, was decidedly American.

"It's good to meet you. My, this is a first for me—talking to detectives instead of running the other way. I guess I'm coming up in the world."

"You certainly look as though you are," Weston noticed approvingly. "Professor Chester must have done a super job in working with you."

"Oh, he did!" She smiled sweetly and turned

around like a fashion model displaying a dress. "This girl used to weigh ninety pounds and spend most of her time 'spaced out.' How's that for a change!"

"Quite impressive," Geoffrey assured her. "I'm interested in the techniques that James employed. Could you give me a brief description?"

June became more serious. Her brown eyes widened slightly, and the Spanish (or was it Italian) cast of her features became noticeable.

"It's not very pleasant to think back upon, but I'll do my best." She frowned. "The first thing he did was to get some of my old pictures—from before I began doing drugs—and enlarge them to poster size. Then he filmed me 'popping' a sugar cube. I remember I really looked stupid just sitting there 'stoned.' Then he and some volunteer helpers strapped me into a chair six hours a day for two weeks. When I wasn't doing that, my mother and father had me locked in their attic."

"I think I'm getting the picture," Weston reflected, "but please go on."

"Well, they stuck pills in front of me, but every time I put one to my mouth I got an electric shock. If I swallowed it I got another shock every couple of minutes until I came down from the 'high.' It gave me bad trips. And whenever I was hungry they'd bring out a trash can and ask me to throw away a tab. If I did I got something to eat. If I didnt, I went hungry. While Professor Chester was out of the room, the poster was always in place to look at. That hideous film was on a screen right beside it."

"And I assume," Geoffrey interrupted, "that you were praised lavishly by everyone whenever you made a right choice."

"Oh, absolutely. In spite of it being a real drag for me, I knew everyone cared. That's what kept me from going completely out of my mind. Later on I was taken out to parties by some really nice guys. I got to meet new people. And there was even a group of ex-junkies that had meetings together. I've still got a telephone number of one of them in my purse."

At this point Twigg broke gruffly into the conversation.

"Did you sign anything to allow this bizarre treatment?"

"Oh, yes. And so did my parents. I knew the way I was living was messing me up, and I wanted to stop."

"Was the college," Weston prodded, "involved at all in your care?"

"No. They didn't know anything about it."

My colleague looked at Miss Albey with an expression I couldn't quite fathom. His concern, however, was clear.

"June, we read in some of the professor's anecdoted records that you have had a problem with guilt. What kind of care have you had in that area?"

"Why, Mr. Chester gave me aptitude tests and also recommended I go to charm school. That helped a lot. And he had sessions with me telling me to let go of my guilt feelings. He said I had been shaped by heredity and environment and that everything I'd done was just reaction to a whole bunch of influences. So I shouldn't worry or feel bad. It made good sense."

Geoffrey scooped up some snow and squeezed it into a ball. Then he threw it with all his might at the side of the temporary. He was, to put it mildly, less than overjoyed with Chester's methods. Having vented his anger on the wall he turned once again to our somewhat startled suspect.

"Please forgive the interruption," he begged. "As a psychologist would say, I was sublimating. Now, where were we? Oh, yes. Are you now completely free of guilt feelings?"

The brunette shook her head.

"No, I still have problems there. But the desire for drugs is gone completely. I took a trip after the treatments. And boy was it a 'bummer.' I was in a room, and blood started pouring out of me until it filled up everything. I was swimming and drowning—and my father says I screamed for four hours."

My partner paused to consider. He seemed indecisive about his next words. But finally he simply breathed deeply and spit his feelings out.

"I don't know how to say this, Miss Albey. Maybe I shouldn't even say part of it. You are obviously better off now than before the experience, but I believe that what you went through is the most hideous form of 'behavior modification' I have ever heard of. To put it bluntly, you were brainwashed in the name of science. I'll never agree that the end justifies the means, and I consider Chester's actions deplorable. The man should be horse whipped if he weren't already dead. And with a bedside manner like that, it's amazing he lived as long as he did. Every one of his patients at one time or another must have fervently wanted to strangle him!" Geoffrey caught his breath and resumed at a slower speed—with a greater measure of composure.

"You say you still have guilt feelings. Good for you! You're normal. You're human. Madam, you're guilty. Don't play games and try to rationalize guilt into a myth. It's not. I feel very sorry for you, thinking of the horror you must feel every time you remember your dead baby. But I would feel even greater sorrow if you felt nothing. June, if everyone were allowed to lay all his guilt down before psychology's pseudo-gods of heredity and environment, then no one would be accountable for anything. A man could rape and torture and walk away whistling because he 'wasn't really responsible.' And wouldn't that make this world a hell! Civilization may yet descend beyond freedom and dignity, but don't you be a party to the travesty. Accept your guilt. Accept your responsibility. Weep bitter tears. And seek a remedy, not a rationalization. I only know of one man who has the power to actually forgive sins. You might consider Him."

June Albey gazed at my colleague solemnly.

"You sound very much like my grandmother."

At that moment three other patients arrived in a group. They were accompanied by a grey-haired gentleman with a full beard who appeared to be an instructor. He held out his hand in greeting.

"Good afternoon, gentlemen." His tone was nasal—slightly haughty. "I'm Dr. Aaron Davidson, the head of James Chester's department. And this is Jackson, Cathy, and George. I am sure you won't mind my sitting in on whatever it is you're planning.

"And if we do?" Inspector Twigg asked.

Aaron shrugged.

"Then I'll sit in anyway to protect these youngsters' best interests. You are aware that they are undergoing psychological difficulties, and I don't intend to see them abused."

"Rest assured," my partner advised, "that we will not add to the damage your profession has already inflicted."

The newcomer looked sharply at Weston.

"Do I detect a note of aggression? Have we got a psychology hater on our hands?"

"What do you think?" Geoffrey shot back. "What would you like to think? What answer would be reinforcing to you?"

"Oh, brother!" I complained. "Will you two stop asking questions? In case you haven't noticed, it's still rather cold and I don't fancy wasting time."

"Quite right," Weston agreed. "Actually, doctor, I'm a connoisseur of good psychology. But there jolly well isn't much of that around. And I detest behaviorism. Ah yes, it all has its roots in my childhood—during undergraduate studies at Oxford when I was taught behaviorism using a teaching-machine-style book. It was the most boring, juvenile thing I ever suffered through. I scanned it in the wrong order, ignoring every repetitious direction, and finished at the head of the class."

"And, no doubt, quickly forgot the material," Davidson concluded.

"No more quickly than anyone else. Boredom is hardly an aid to effective study."

The doctor stuffed his hands in his coat pockets and scowled. I hoped he'd drop the subject so that we could get on with the business at hand but he didn't. The temptation to defend his branch of study was just too great.

"And what," he challenged, "do you feel 'good psychology'—as you call it—is?"

"Do you really want to know?" Weston replied. "Or do you merely wish to debate?"

Aaron paused uneasily. He wasn't used to having his questions bounce back.

"I'd . . . like to know."

"Wonderful." Geoffrey looked past Davidson to the students as he spoke. "The word is derived from Greek terms meaning 'knowledge of the soul or spirit.' Good psychology leaves room for a soul in man. It neither treats him as a computer nor as a mere animal. It sees social influences, but it holds everyone personally accountable for his actions."

"That," the doctor interrupted, "I can agree with—to a point. Your spirit idea is rather fanciful, but one does have to leave room for ethics. I tend to shop around and mix the thoughts of several schools myself."

"Good show," Weston complimented him.

"Behaviorism has added some important concepts to learning theory, but it becomes absurd if viewed as *the school.* It's simply made some good discoveries in spite of basic flaws. But other schools are equally in error. Good psychology, professor, rejects Lock's blank slate theory. I agree that little Julia does not make conscious choices when she is first born. But by the time her reason is functional, she has already developed so many habits centered around her own way, that she continues to enforce her selfish tendencies until she becomes solidly fixed as the focal point of her universe. This has not resulted from the corrupting influence of her parents either. She may at times actually drive *them* up the wall! Good psychology doesn't pit parent against child or use the one as an excuse for the other, although there are undoubtedly influences in *both* directions. And decent psychology doesn't turn the devil into a myth or change man into a cherub. I'm OK and you're OK and we're all becoming people. Balderdash! We aren't the good seeking improvement. We're sinners seeking to have our own way. The new self-help schools lionize man so much they almost make him an idol!"

"Do you then," Davidson suggested sarcastically, "suggest that we go all the way back to Freud?"

Geoffrey stamped his feet against the cold.

"Of course not. The man treated too many hysterical women who had sexual problems. It warped his theories. And he was dead wrong in seeing Satan as a mere projection of a person's father. But I'll give him credit for one thing. He saw evil. Isn't it amazing how the trend has shifted away from that in recent years?"

"I can see," the doctor thought aloud, "how a detective like yourself would have a negative view of people. You rather specialize on the seamy side of life, don't you?"

"Actually," Geoffrey disagreed, "I have a realistic view. And my being a detective has nothing to do with it. My being a Christian IS a factor. And good psychology will leave room for Christ in the healing process—whether the problem is anxiety, obsession or a poor self-image."

Dr. Davidson pursed his lips as though Weston's last statement explained everything. He spoke now in his most reasonable bedside manner.

"So you're a mystic. And you're upset that some of our concepts are at odds with your religious views. Don't be too harsh on us. We see the value of religious experience in integrating a personality. And we are dealing, after all, with the secular world. Your point of view is valid for you. I accept that. I simply ask you to be open-minded and not to condemn ours."

I groaned aloud at that answer. The doctor had literally tossed a red cape in front of a bull. Even Twigg rolled his eyes at the man's technique.

"Come on, fellows," I broke in quickly. "Stop this 'non-debate.' We'll be here all day and there's work to do."

"Just a minute, John," Weston waved me off. "I have a few more statements to make and then we'll stop." He turned sternly to the psychologist.

"Doctor, I spoke to the issues. I didn't attack you personally. But you have used nothing but 'poisoning the well' tactics. You imply I'm a narrow-minded religionist. But you have shown the narrow mind. Religion is to you merely an experience to be used clinically. You don't care if it's true or not. By implication, you doubt that it is. And you're willing to fracture *truth* into a thousand little relative, existential half-truths: 'This is true for you, but that is true for me.' Well, I can't accept that. My very job is the separating of facts from opinions. And you'd better base your profession on absolutes, too. If you don't, you descend into an amoral swamp from which there is no escape. What's 'normal' becomes determined by a poll, and deviate behavior gains automatic acceptability as soon as enough people are warped in that direction. And who's to say you're above doing some warping yourself? Chester's Pavlovian antics are a case in point." He gestured to the students with his arms. "How many of you at one time or another absolutely hated James Chester? Raise your hands so the doctor can see the beauty of 'pure' science."

June Albey's arm shot up immediately, followed by that of George Singleton who, along with Hill, had arrived in the midst of the discussion.

"Put those hands down," Davidson commanded. "Don't you see he's trying to get you to implicate yourselves. If Jim's really dead, you might end up in gaol."

Several had started to raise their hands but lowered them again at the doctor's words. June and George, arms still held high, looked at each other uneasily.

Geoffrey smiled and motioned them down.

"It looks, doctor, as though James Chester was not quite as popular as everyone at first assumed. But these people aren't indicted by their admission. Chester's actions *are.* And I sincerely hope you'll take that to heart."

"Many patients," Aaron assured him coolly, "either love or hate their psychologist during the treatment process. You have proven exactly nothing. And, come to think of it, you haven't even shown that Jim is dead. George was telling me on the way here that he saw the man the day after you seem to think he was killed. Is that right?"

"Oh, that!" Weston snapped his half-frozen fingers. "I have an item that you should find interesting." He searched his coat pockets and finally extracted what looked like a garage door opener. "If you will be so good as to press the 'on' button, doctor, you will discover how the killer provided his victim with an alibi."

With a good deal of hauteur Aaron took the device and jabbed the controls. I don't know what I expected—a flash of light, a hypnotic voice wooing us to sleep. Nothing happened.

"Well?" the doctor mused. "What does that prove? That you're a complete crackpot?"

My colleague smiled disarmingly.

"It might seem that way at first, I'll have to agree. But if you look over there behind your back—through James' window—I think . . . "

Twigg gasped.

"It can't be, Geoff! How did you do it?"

There was a man seated in Chester's office—in front of the desk. And, ignoring the smoking cigar in the ash tray, he was slowly leafing his way through a pile of papers. I would have recognized him anywhere. It was . . . GEOFFREY WESTON!

"If you'll accompany me inside," my partner promised nonchalantly, "I'll show you how it's done."

He hardly had the words out before Singleton was on the run toward the building. Jackson Smyth, a brutish-looking fellow was second—followed by the rest. Remembering his dignity, Twigg hung back slightly from the stampede. Aaron, Geoff, and I took up the rear. Weston was whistling.

By the time we arrived, everyone was gathered around either the strange looking machine squatting on the filing cabinet or the even odder figure by the desk. The man sitting there didn't have any back to him! From the window he might look normal, but he was only half of an empty shell!

My colleague strode confidently into the room. "Well, people, what do you make of it?"

"It's a blimey projection!" Smyth declared as he ran his hand effortlessly through the seated figure. "I saw a machine like that on the telly once."

"Not," Geoffrey assured him, "quite like that." He walked to the filing cabinet and pointed with a touch of pride to the projector. "The holographic image that this device produces is something entirely different from anything achieved before. You'd never know it from television fiction, but up until now all such pictures have been monochromatic—one color. That's why I asked the witnesses yesterday if they'd noticed any unusual lighting when they saw Chester. They, of course, hadn't. Previous images have also been still lifes. This machine, as you've noticed, allows for limited movement—not to much, or the figure goes out of focus."

Twigg surveyed the projector dubiously.

"How does it work, Weston? And *why* was it used?"

"The first answer," my partner noted, "is rather technical. But I'll try to give you a rough idea. To take the picture, the colored beams of the pulse laser are split. One half of each beam bounces off the subject and exposes a frame of film. The other half is deflected to the same film by a mirror—creating an odd pattern of whirls, or interference marks. The machine in front of you reverses the process and reproduces the interference patterns in mid air." He indicated the three tubes sticking out of the projector. "The picture is in color because each of these emits a different frequency laser light. It's very similar to the way the electron guns work in an old-style color television tube."

"That's as clear as mud," I observed. "Last night you still had several theories in the running. What made you decide on this one?"

Weston unbuttoned his coat and pulled out a bag of peanuts. He ripped open the cellophane before speaking.

"Actually, John, there were three reasons. The first, as I've mentioned to you before, was the absence of odor. But the other two were of far greater significance."

"And they were?" I prompted.

"The presence of smoke and the absence of dust."

At this point Aaron Davidson, who had become pretty much of a spectator, broke into the conversation.

"I think I see part of what you're driving at. With an image that big and employing film, there is bound to be a resolution problem."

"Excellent, Doctor!" Geoffrey eyed the professor with renewed respect. "At first the smoke bothered me. If there were a projection, I reasoned that the smoke would appear only in the area the projector focused on. The room wouldn't be filled—as all the witnesses had claimed. But then I realized the obvious. Only the area around the desk was brightly lighted—by the desk lamp. And all the action was taking place there. No one would notice or perhaps even be able to see that the shadows were clear. The smoke served a very important function. It concealed any graininess or minute distortions in the holographic image.

"The absence of dust on top of the filing cabinet was also suggestive—particularly since that area of the room is not visible from the window. Something had been placed there. And a dust rag was used to remove any tell-tale imprints. That one piece of physical evidence caused me to reject my other theories . . . once I discovered that a pro-

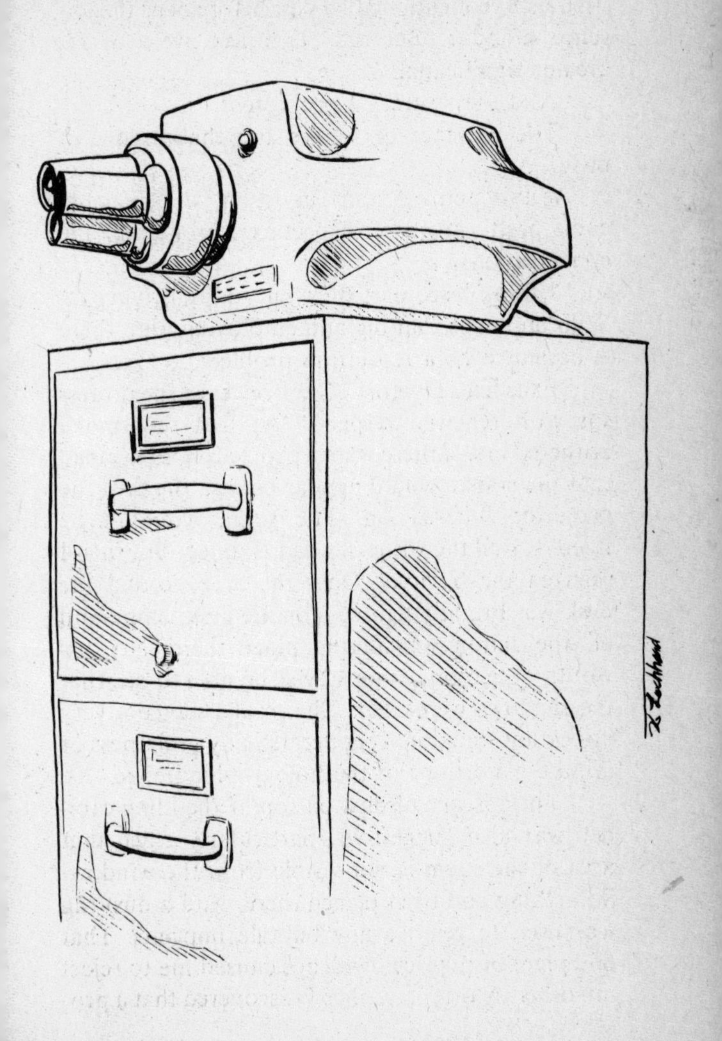

jector such as the one you see here actually existed.

"But," I protested, "if we saw a film, why didn't Chester's cigar get shorter?"

Geoffrey popped a handful of peanuts into his mouth. He was enjoying himself.

"John, holographic motion pictures are very ticklish to make. I mentioned the focusing problem. Speckles may also appear on the image. I worked all night with a laboratory assistant for one usable production, and it's only ten minutes long. I believe the murderer only got two or three minutes of good footage, made copies, and started splicing. You've seen the old Felix the cat cartoons where the same action is repeated again and again."

"But," Twigg pointed out, "that brings us back to my second question—which you neglected to answer. Why would the murderer go to all the trouble? Why wouldn't he have simply dumped the corpse in the crematory and forgotten about it? I don't see any point to the whole charade."

"I've put a good deal of thought into that," Weston admitted. "To my knowledge there are only five prototypes of this machine in existence. And it was neither easy nor safe to steal one of them."

"You're sure," I asked, "that it was stolen?"

"Oh, yes—some four months ago from the National Physical Laboratory in Teddington. And the murderer must have had a reason for taking the risk. There's only one possibility that I can think of. And I hope I'm wrong."

"You believe," the answer suddenly dawned

on me, "that this is only the first of several murders! That's why we were at Faversham this morning."

"Precisely," Geoffrey acknowledged. "The murderer knew that for some reason the future victims would suspect they were next in line if they heard about a killing. So he tried to disguise it—without knowing, of course, about Chester's chrome joint. He thought the man would be presumed to have simply disappeared without a trace the day after the crematorium incident."

"In that case," the Inspector scowled, "we have our work cut out for us. Do you have any clues as to who the killer might be?"

Weston paused to survey each person in the group. Several could not maintain eye contact.

"Only, Inspector, that if one person acted alone he (or she) was relatively strong, knew how to drive, was a good friend of Chester's, and enjoyed a confidential, professional relationship with him."

"How on earth," Singleton exclaimed, "can you tell all that from the little bit o' dust what's missing from the cabinet?"

"Yes," I agreed. "I'd like to hear that, too."

Geoffrey seemed pleased at our inquisitiveness.

"It's elementary, really." He gestured toward the machine. "One simply cannot make a holographic record without the subject knowing about it. Laser beams trained on a person tend to give the show away. So we must assume that Chester—not realizing the killer's intentions—was a party to the filming. But if he was, he didn't even tell his wife about it. I asked her last night. I conclude, therefore, that he viewed the filming as being in some way confidential. The 'photographer' must have been an employer, colleague, or perhaps a patient."

Our invited guests looked at one another—trying to guess who the murderer might be. Jason Phelps, a weak-chinned youngster with glasses, raised his hand hesitantly as though he were in class and wanted Geoffrey to call on him.

"Sir," he stammered, "I was at home with Mother Monday night. That's when George tells me the cremation happened. If you want to, you can ask her."

"I appreciate your openness," Geoffrey assured him in a kindly manner. "We'll do just that. Is there anyone else who has an alibi for late Monday night?"

"I was up until two studying," Jackson Smyth volunteered.

"Very commendable," my partner observed. "Was anyone with you?"

The burly collegian shook his head disappointedly.

"How about you?" Weston gestured toward Davidson. "Do you have an alibi for the date in question?"

"Me!"

I thought the good doctor would gag. He was positively thunderstruck.

"Why I came here to protect the students!"

"And now," Geoffrey declared wryly, "you've graduated from busybody to suspect. Where were you Monday night?"

"I was," he replied, "asleep in bed with my wife. Where else would I be?"

"Where else, indeed. Was she asleep, too?"

"Of course . . . "

Geoffrey eyed Aaron with mock suspicion.

"How do you know?"

"How do I know what?" the professor asked testily.

"That she was asleep."

"Why . . . " he floundered in confusion. "I mean I presume that she was asleep. I can't know, obviously, if I was asleep myself."

"That's true," Geoffrey agreed. "And she can't know if you were there either. I'm afraid, Aaron, that you've managed to retain suspect status."

Inspector Twigg cleared his throat.

"Geoff, now that we've established that alibis don't grow on trees around here, will you please tell us why you believe the murderer was well-muscled and drove a motorcar."

"Oh, certainly," my colleague replied. "I do seem to get side-tracked, don't I? Actually a motorcar had to be involved in the killing. James Chester was intercepted somewhere between the college and his house. That means he was probably offered a ride by someone he trusted. The alternative, that he was bumped on the head and then dragged down the street, simply won't do. Half the city would have seen the murderer."

"But," I suggested, "James could have stopped off at a friend's house on the way home."

Weston stroked his goatee in thought.

"Yes, that's true enough . . . But even so, the killer would have had to haul the body to the cemetery. Once there, even a strong man or woman would not have found it an easy task to lift the corpse over the wall and drag it to the crematorium. Our killer *if acting alone* had to know how to drive and to have some athletic ability."

Aaron scratched his beard.

"That still doesn't tell us very much, Mr. Weston. Jason is the only one here to my knowledge that doesn't drive. And even the weakest of us could have had accomplices."

"Absolutely," Weston concurred. "And I'm not limiting our list of potential assassins to those in this room." He turned to the Inspector. "Twigg, I want you to interview every professor that works in this building. Find out who was on good terms with Chester and who wasn't. I'd like the information as soon as possible." My colleague then looked in turn at each of the students. His gaze was penetrating, almost intimidating. "Ladies and gentlemen, if you think of anything—anything at all—about this case that you haven't mentioned, get in touch with either myself or the Inspector. And be VERY careful these next few days. If you like, I'm sure Twigg would put you in protective custody. Remember that the murderer may have plans to kill again. And YOU may be his next victim. If the Inspector doesn't have further business with you, you're free to go now."

Twigg shook his head and addressed the gathering.

"I don't have anything to add, except that we'll expect everyone to remain in the area." He pulled a stack of business cards from his wallet. "Here's my number in case any of you need to speak with me in the future." He handed the pile to a student who took a card and passed the rest on.

The room now erupted in general conversation as everyone prepared to leave. Jason Phelps and Cathy Hopkins, the two nervous, bird-like members of the group, came over to speak with Twigg. I guessed that they were seriously considering Geoffrey's offer of protective custody. As I unplugged the projector and started packing it away, I noticed that Davidson had also attracted a following. June Albey, Stephen Hill and Jackson Smyth were engaging him in an animated conversation as they passed through the door. By the time the machine had cooled down and been stuffed in the box, the room was empty—except for four drab walls, a battered desk, and a lot of memories.

"Where," I asked Weston, "do we go from here?"

My partner picked up the other end of the box.

"I don't know about you, John, but after we drop the projector off I'm going back to Baker Street. There isn't an awful lot we can do right now. And when things start popping, I want to be rested."

"What do you mean 'start popping'?"

Geoffrey stifled a yawn.

"We'll know that, my friend, when it happens."

Without speaking further, we carried the box out to the Mercedes. The trip home—which included a detour all the way to South London—took slightly over an hour.

CHAPTER 6

Monkey on the Back

As soon as we stepped into our quarters, I knew we had a problem. Gladstone had not been supplied with one of the necessities of indoor living! As I opened windows to air the place out, Geoffrey put one of our clue envelopes to a new use. Shortly after that, the apartment once again approached livability. My partner retired to his bedroom. I imported a box of loam from the garden and Gladstone reclined on the rocker—watching the whole affair with bored disinterest.

Cooking is not one of my pleasures. So I scanned the icebox for leftovers. I found some oxtail soup and ran across four baked Spanish onions. The menu was complete. While dinner simmered on the top burner, I read the lead articles in *The Daily Telegraph*. It looked as though the world might hold together until morning—just barely. The King had officiated at another ceremony. The Middle East was in its usual turmoil. And Parliament had just banned catalytic converters for causing ground pollution. When I said grace I thanked the Lord for the food and for His patience in putting up with us all.

The three-day-old soup tasted better than it had originally—perhaps because I was hungrier. And a glass of milk really hit the spot. After finishing a leisurely lunch, I poured a bowl of milk for the cat, and started washing the dishes. Luckily, however, the doorbell rescued me from the dishwater.

"Just a moment! I'm coming."

As I walked through the living room, I picked up our coats from the back of a chair and tossed them into the closet. The bell rang again. Obviously someone was impatient.

"Hold onto your hat!"

Pushing the button that unlocked the front gate, I then unlatched the door. As it swung open I greeted a young lady walking toward me in a familiar Eskimo coat. She seemed just as cheerful as before—though a trifle miffed at our security system. Her greeting was bantering.

"Mr. Taylor, is this a house you have or a prison?"

"It depends on the weather," I assured her. "Come on in."

As she walked past I reached out my hand to help her off with her coat. Underneath all that fur she turned out to be quite slender.

"Actually," I added, "the iron work out front was installed while the Irish Republicans were still running around. But in our profession we find it useful. Have a seat and I'll get you some hot tea. It will just take a second."

"You're very kind." June smiled gratefully as she set about rubbing her numb hands.

I put her coat on an end table and retreated to the kitchen. When I returned with two steaming cups, she was in an easy chair and looking around the living room with evident curiosity. Casually dressed in a blouse and jeans, she seemed both alert and relaxed.

"This," I gestured expansively (almost spilling the tea), "is our 'Victoria's scientific, Danish, Early-American' motif. It's designed to inspire imagination—from the bunsen burners and pipets in that corner, to the colonial wall clock, to the modern stereo over there. Our interior decorator was hurricane Celia."

Miss Albey laughed and tossed her dark brown hair back over her shoulders.

"It's not exactly 'establishment,' " she contributed. "I like it. You fellows must do an awful lot of reading."

"We do for a fact. The detective business is a little like the army. There's a lot of 'hurry up and wait' connected with it." I set the cup and saucer, with a couple of lumps of sugar, on the arm of her chair. "But I'm sure you didn't come here just to talk about our leisure activities."

"No," she admitted, "I didn't. Mr. Weston said something this afternoon that really started me thinking, and I wanted to talk to him about it. I called the Inspector and he gave me your address. I hope you don't mind."

"Not in the least. But unfortunately Geoffrey is indisposed at the moment. He was up all night working on the case and is trying to catch up on his sleep. Perhaps I could be of help."

June's smile faded. She did not seem at all convinced.

"I hope so, Mr. Taylor. This is very important to me."

"Please call me John."

"If you like." She paused and bit her lip. "John, I'm nearly twenty-four . . . and feel like I've tried everything. If you've looked at Professor Chester's records you know I haven't exactly grown up in an ivory tower."

I sat down in a chair across from her and took a sip of tea.

"There are very few ivory towers being built these days, Miss Albey. Please go on."

"Well . . . I don't want to be disappointed again, that's all."

Her manner was composed—resolute. But I sensed hidden scars and could almost feel the shallowness that she had lived through.

"I understand," I spoke softly. "You're here because of what Geoffrey said about forgiveness and Jesus Christ."

"Yes." June looked down at her blue jeans without really seeing them. "And because of something old man Davidson told me after that. He claims that people invented religion as a crutch because they couldn't face reality."

"No doubt," I ventured, "you would like some proof one way or another."

"Right on. If there's any real meaning to my life, I want to know what it is. If there's none, well . . ."

"I understand. And I'll try to answer you—

although volumes have been written on the subject by my betters." I leaned forward in the chair. "Will you do something for me?"

"What?" There was a note of hesitancy in her reply.

"Simply bow your head," I encouraged, "and ask God to help me say the right things."

"I guess I can do that," she brightened. "But I'll feel awfully foolish if I find out later He doesn't exist."

"Take the risk."

"What shall I say?" She started chewing on her nails. "I mean I've never done anything like this before."

I shrugged my shoulders.

"June, simply say what's on your heart."

The room was quiet now except for the ticking of the clock, the crackling of flames in the fire-place, and the muffled passage of motorcars out front. My visitor bowed her head and stammered a simple, honest prayer. And I said a silent "amen" to her request. When she had finished I got up to put a couple of logs on the fire, then returned to my chair.

"Now, young lady, let's get down to business. First there's the matter of Davidson's theory." I paused a moment to reflect. "I suppose it sounds convincing on the surface. Primitive man feared fire, thunder and lightning. And it would be comforting to him to decide they were gods, pretend they had human emotions, and try to get them on his side. There may even be an element of that in the roots of the simple nature religions. But

Davidson is oversimplifying and distorting." I pointed my finger at her. "Let me explain.

"Say you want to buy a motorcar. You pay your money. You drive it home. But then a blind friend comes up to you who doesn't believe in motorcars. And he says, 'You need to travel, so your mind has invented a non-existent vehicle to give you confidence.' What would your reaction be?"

June, arms propped under her chin, had been paying close attention. She raised her cup to her lips now before replying.

"Why, I would say he was as mad as those people I read about who believe in a flat earth."

"Precisely. But could you convince him he was wrong? You might force him to touch your motorcar. You might give him a ride. But if he were totally convinced that the object were fictitious, he would doubt his senses rather than his theory. I believe that is what Aaron Davidson has done with God. There's no way the man could be satisfied. If the Lord fulfills a need in man, then He's automatically a human fiction. If He doesn't, then no one—including Davidson—would want Him! Heads the professor wins; tails God loses. What Aaron is really saying (with the scientific wrapping paper cut away) is, 'Since I don't believe God exists, mankind must have invented Him to do all the good they think He does.' "

Miss Albey pursed her lips and frowned.

"I see where you're coming from. But that still doesn't prove people didn't invent God."

"No, it doesn't," I agreed. "But let's specifically look at the Christian religion. What is the God of the Bible like? Is He a nice, fun-loving chap who winks at our sins, likes a little 'hanky panky' himself and keeps conveniently out of the way when we don't want Him around? Not one whit! Pagan deities may be 'father images' that reflect man's flawed nature. But the God of the Old and New Testaments is a very different, holy sort of Father. He has an absolute set of laws. He has stoked up an eternal lake of fire for the wicked. And He is *EVERYWHERE* watching.

"Let's be personal for a moment, June. Think of the one act in your life that gives you the greatest sense of shame. Close your eyes and visualize it."

She paused to consider.

"That's quite an order, Mr. Taylor. There are several in the running. I guess . . . O.K. At least this one is near the top." She squeezed her eyelids shut. "I'm picturing it."

"Good. Now imagine that you can see the Holy God there all around you recording every detail—down to your very thoughts. Would you invent that kind of God?"

Miss Albey crinkled her nose in disgust.

"Certainly not. If I thought God was like that, it would blow my mind! I wouldn't be able to face myself in the mirror again."

"Precisely. Atheists might rationalize and say that such a being didn't exist, but no one would ever invent Him. And no one did. HE IS REAL. I believe there's reality behind the pagan deities also—but of a different sort. Paul said they were demons. And that makes sense. If a religion had no supernatural power at all behind it, sooner or later people would notice the lack and wander away. Satan has his evil substitutes for the real thing—carefully tailored to appeal to man's animal nature.

"June, psychology may have been invented by man to meet his own emotional needs, but the Christian God has always existed. I believe His work of design can be seen in every flower, every microscopic animal, every star—even in the interworkings of your own body. And His wisdom has been put into words. Hundreds of years before Christ He spoke through prophets promising to send His Son, the God-Man, to be born of a virgin in Bethlehem, to speak out against evil, to be crucified for your sin, to have nails driven into Him, to die with wicked men, to be buried in a rich man's tomb, and to conquer death. It all happened as promised—point by point."

My guest had been following me up to this time. But now a look of puzzlement crossed her face.

"But why would He bother? If He's as stern and just as you say, then I'm only some ugly little insect to be squashed."

"No," I disagreed. "You're anything but that. Have you ever seen an oriental painting? The figures are tiny, but the artist loved them into being. And the 'everywhere God' did the same to you and me. He really cares about us. That's why He sent His Son. If we see our ugliness, give up on ourselves, and cling to Jesus in trust, then the Lord can be righteous and still forgive us. The price of justice was paid on the cross."

June shook her head.

"I don't know, Mr. . . . John. That last part sounds really beautiful. If I could only believe that . . . "

The gravelly jangle of the telephone took us both by surprise. I wondered, as I got awkwardly to my feet, who it might be. Twigg, perhaps. Not that many people had our unlisted number.

"Remember what you were about to say," I advised Miss Albey over my shoulder as I walked across the room. "Hopefully we'll get back to it in a moment." As the telephone started to ring again I picked up the receiver.

"Hallo. Sleuths Limited of Baker Street. Taylor speaking."

It *was* the Inspector, and he sounded excited.

"John, get Geoffrey for me at once! And hurry it up."

"Hold on a moment." I clunked the receiver onto the table, strode to the doorway, and shouted down the hall. "Geoff, Filbert is on the phone and he's having kittens. Put something on and come on out here. Dress for company. There's a lady visiting." In answer I could hear my colleague banging around in the bedroom. In just a few seconds he came hurrying into view, shirttail flopping down over his trousers and eyelids forced open by a new flow of adrenalin. Not so much as glancing at our guest, he grabbed the phone and spoke in clipped tones.

"Yes, Inspector, what is it? . . . He has what!

. . . Yes, that is amazing . . . Of course we want to. We'll be waiting out front. This is important, Twigg. Have them give him another transfusion. Yes, I mean it. And check for poison! Good day."

When Geoffrey turned toward us his face had drained of color. Shock, intense disappointment, and sorrow intermingled.

"John," he stated levelly, "thirty minutes ago Bertram Seawell was stabbed twice in the back *by a monkey*. They've got the man over at St. Bartholomew's right now operating on him. Twigg will be here momentarily to pick us up. That's his siren in the distance."

I was almost too stunned to speak.

"I say. . . . You can't mean it! By a . . . monkey. This case is getting more bizarre by the minute Did you—"

"There isn't time to speculate right now. Say good-bye to the lady while I get ready for the street."

He turned on his heels and walked—almost ran—back down the hall, leaving me alone once again with Miss Albey. She drained her cup and got lithely to her feet.

"You don't have to show me to the door, John. I know this is an emergency. Who is the man, anyway?"

"One of Professor Chester's friends." I pulled a couple of volumes down from the bookcase and held them out to her.

"Here, take these. They may answer some questions we never got to. Do come back. And . . . be careful. I should hate to hear that anything awful happened to you."

She finished sliding into her coat and looked very seriously into my face. As she reached forward to take the books, she surprised me with a quick kiss on the cheek.

"You're a good man, John Taylor. I believe you really would feel bad." She turned and walked briskly to the door.

"Push the button on the jam," I called after her, "or you'll never get out of the gate."

* * * * *

We sped down Oxford Street—the two-tone beep of the siren clearing a path in front of us. Inspector Nolan was driving. Geoffrey and I were in the back seat, and Twigg was sitting up front venting his spleen.

"Geoff, that was the most stupid move you've ever made. And you two have made some dandies! Your circus tactics may have just cost a man his life. I hope you realize that! When you talked to Seawell you should have had the decency to let us know about it. We could have put the man under surveillance. We could have staked out his house. But no. You hit and run and leave the man at the mercy of the killer. We wouldn't have even connected him to the Chester case if he hadn't called the locals this morning claiming that *you* had threatened him!"

Geoffrey was more subdued than I had seen him in a long while. He didn't seem angered in the slightest by the Inspector's outburst. But I was.

"Twigg," I retaliated, "will you please start thinking rationally? We should have told you about Seawell. I'll grant you that. But I did mention our trip to Faversham, and you should have known—"

"I should have known! I'm supposed to be following up clues as to the activities of detectives? It's not enough I should be tracking down criminals!"

"Will you two," Weston broke in softly, "please stop bickering? This is a time for the mind—not the mouth. Inspector, what's done is done. And I apologize for it. But we spoke with nearly a dozen people. And I know you didn't watch them all. Neither you nor I could have singled Bertram out as the next victim. Even if he had been placed under surveillance, it would not have prevented the knifing. The monkey was already inside the house. No, what we have to do now is discover if there are yet other victims."

"Other victims!" Twigg slapped his forehead in consternation. "You don't really expect this madness to continue, do you?"

"I do. I think the murderer had planned to act at a leisurely pace without alarming his prey. But we called his hand by exposing Chester's murder for what it was. Now the bodies may fall like bowling pins unless we do something quickly."

"And what," I asked, "do you propose that we do?"

Geoffrey put his hands behind his neck and stretched.

"Think. Just think."

The conversation withered as the reality of the situation dawned on each of us. Geoffrey was right. There might be further violence. And we couldn't adequately protect the dozen potential victims we knew of now—let alone those that might pop up in coming days. Seawell was the key. If only he survived long enough and had some idea as to who his assassin was! Nolan made a skidding turn onto King Edward Street, and we came to a sudden stop in front of the emergency entrance.

As the four of us walked inside, Twigg flashed his badge at the first orderly we saw and demanded to be taken to Bertram. Thus enlisted, the young man checked some records and led our procession down a spotless, white corridor past three operating rooms. We came to a stop in front of a door marked "Post. Op." and waited impatiently while our guide went in to speak with the resident intern. Almost immediately the extra-wide panel opened with a "wushing" sound and we were confronted by a white-smocked gentleman in his early thirties. The tell-tale spatter of red across his front spoke worlds about his afternoon activities.

"May I help you, gentlemen?"

"Yes." Twigg spoke with authority. "I'm from the Yard, and we're here on official business. We would like to speak with Mr. Seawell."

"I'm afraid that won't be possible right now. He's just coming out of the anesthesia, and the fellow had an awfully rough time of it."

"That badly injured," Nolan sympathized. "How long will we have to wait?"

"Actually," the doctor corrected, "the knife wounds weren't serious at all. One slid along the rib cage and the other missed any vital organs. But the poison really put him in a bad way. It's a good thing you gentlemen called when you did, or we would have lost him. Even now I can't promise anything. It will take a few days for us to determine the full extent of damage."

"That," Weston remarked with urgency, "is time we don't have. Wouldn't it be possible for us to see him for just a moment or so? Someone else's life may depend on it."

The surgeon looked doubtful, then shrugged.

"It won't do him any harm, I suppose. You may see him for a few seconds. But don't be surprised if you don't learn anything. He'll be fairly groggy."

So saying, he pushed the door back and ushered us in. The pungent odor of disinfectant was heavy in the air, and sterile equipment glittered from wall to wall. After putting on masks we approached the patient. He was lying on his stomach with tubes leading into his nose and arms. Bertram was no longer the pompous showman, but a helpless, obese hulk fighting for every breath. I noticed Weston shake his head in pity. Twigg, however, was hardened to the sight— having witnessed far more violence during his years on the force than either Geoffrey or I. He leaned over the victim with quiet insistence.

"Mr. Seawell, do you hear me?"

"Yeesss." The word was so rasping and throaty that we could hardly make it out.

"I'm Inspector Twigg of Scotland Yard. Do you know who did this to you?"

"C . . . c . . . can't say." Bertram gasped convulsively for breath. Beads of perspiration ran off his back onto the paper beneath.

Now it was my partner's turn to bend down.

"Mr. Seawell, this is Geoffrey Weston. Do you have any idea who the next victim might be?"

Our only answer was the sound of heavy breathing. Geoffrey tried again.

"Please think hard. Is there anyone at all who is associated with both you and Chester?"

"H . . . Hugh . . . Ev . . . ans."

At this point the doctor pushed us away from the table.

"I'm sorry, gentlemen, but that will be enough questioning for now. I think you've gotten all the—"

Bertram's hoarse whisper started up again.

"W . . . West . . . on you'rre r . . . r . . . right. Af . . . raid tooo d . . . die. B . . . ut c . . c . . . can't . . . be . . . lieve."

I maneuvered past the intern and put my mouth to Seawell's ear.

"Yes, you can, old chap. You can! Do it before it's too late."

" . . . too . . . late . . . "

He started heaving and groaning in pain. And I was pulled gently away. In a moment we were back out in the hall plotting our next move. Twigg and Nolan rushed for a telephone to find out if Hugh Evans was employed by Consolidated Cryogenics. Geoffrey went to the visiting room in hopes of spying Mrs. Seawell. And I . . . I dried my eyes with my handkerchief.

CHAPTER 7

Fire on Ice

The lawn behind St. Bartholomew's was still covered with thick-crusted snow, although plows and salt had cleared the nearby roads. The temperature was dropping again and shadows were lengthening. More flakes were expected by midnight. Twigg, Weston and I were huddled in the middle of the field—waiting.

"I hope," the Inspector complained, "that the dispatcher didn't make a mistake. It's way overdue."

"Ten minutes," Weston corrected, "is hardly 'way' anything. The helicopter was probably on traffic patrol and had to refuel before coming. Here, have some peanuts and settle down. Inspector Nolan is taking steps to protect Consolidated's employees. The authorities in Wales have been notified. And we'll be at the foot of Snowden in slightly over an hour. Everything is under control."

Twigg accepted the nuts and tossed a handful into his mouth.

"Yes, I suppose you're right. But it certainly would have simplified matters if Evans hadn't gone off on vacation this weekend."

"That," I pointed out, "remains to be seen. The man might be dead by now if he hadn't left town."

A faint "wump, wump" sound could soon be heard to the south of us. Turning toward the sound we soon sighted a speck on the horizon moving in our direction. A few seconds later it was the size of a dragonfly and still growing.

As the helicopter landed the three of us ran toward it, backs hunched over to avoid the blast from the whirling blades. Instead the rotarwash kicked the icy snow up into our faces, biting and stinging with the force of a sandblaster. I felt a good deal of relief when we reached the safety of the cockpit. No sooner had we fastened our seat belts before the pilot pulled back on the throttle and the craft was airborne. Buildings shrank rapidly beneath us and took on the appearance of tiny matchbox houses. The craft made a banking turn and headed toward the northwest—still gaining in altitude. It was difficult to speak or even to think above the throb of the engine.

"When," I shouted at Twigg, "are we going to get the results of your snooping? I haven't seen a single Yard report since we started this case!"

"All in good time, mate. You don't need the material on the witnesses anymore since the holographics demonstration. And we're still doing a workup on the college staff and Chester's patients."

"What do you mean we don't need it? We asked for it, didn't we?"

"I don't think Filbert knew whether I was serious or not.

"Of course you asked for it. Good grief, I'll send it over as soon as we get back to London! Does that satisfy you? On second thought . . ."

"Here it comes," Geoffrey predicted. "I think we're about to be blackmailed."

Inspector Twigg grinned broadly at Weston.

"Indeed you are, old chap. Let's exchange that report for, say, an explanation of how you knew Seawell had been poisoned."

"Fair enough," my colleague shot back. "I knew that knives have two sides and monkeys don't play 'mumblety-peg.' "

The Inspector groaned.

"If I wanted a riddle, Weston, I would be reading a book instead of sitting in this helicopter with two fanatics."

"Heavenmobile," I corrected."

"What?"

"As a fanatic," I teased, "I've never liked the word 'helicopter.' Sounds slightly demonic, don't you think? 'Heavenmobile' is a vast improvement."

Twigg looked as though he would burst a blood vessel.

"Why me?" he thought aloud. "With all the places I could be right now, I have to be stuffed between a clown and a court jester at six thousand feet!"

"Actually," Weston continued in a more serious vein, "it was a simple matter to deduce the presence of poison. Chimpanzees are not exactly adept in their use of knives. And when the murderer programmed the animal to attack Seawell, he really couldn't count on a lethal thrust. Since Bertram's walls are lined with knives, it was obvious someone had smeared them with death insurance."

"But the maid," I protested, "would have—"

"She would have dusted only one side of the blades, John. It would be terribly time consuming to take them down and clean them piece by piece. And the killer knew that."

"That leaves us," the Inspector reflected gloomily, "with only the question of how the murderer whispered orders into the monkey's ear."

Geoffrey turned his head to look down at the countryside. Buildings were beginning to light up here and there as evening approached.

"I fancy," he remarked casually, "that was easy enough. Mrs. Seawell tells me that Bertram received a telephone call just before the attack. The caller must have maneuvered him into saying some key word that triggered the animal's conditioning." Weston closed his eyes and relaxed. "I'll expect that report, Filbert, within half an hour of our return to the city."

Soon darkness closed in around us and we hung suspended between two layers of stars. Lights below sprinkled the hills with Christmas glitter. And the sky above displayed its jewels with startling clarity. But we were traveling through shadows—accompanied only by the green glow of the instrument panel. The "wump, wump" of the motor no longer seemed so loud. Now it was more rhythmical and soothing. And the three of us rested in anticipation of a long evening.

* * * * *

I jerked alert without really knowing why. Something had changed. Then I realized that the craft was no longer pitched so far forward. And the 'wush' of the blades had changed its tone. We were angling in for a landing. I shook Twigg back to consciousness, pointing at the same time to some rustic buildings beneath us.

"I say, there's Brookshire Lodge! We'll jolly well find out something now, won't we, Inspector?"

In answer, the Scotland Yarder glared at me and yawned. Still half asleep, he obviously didn't share my enthusiasm. We descended gingerly onto a lighted clearing in front of the largest "cottage." Geoffrey was the first out followed by myself and the Inspector. The snow here was ankle deep and loose. As we struggled toward the cleared walkway, I looked about with the eye of a tourist. Pine forests extended in every direction. And the dim outline of Snowden was barely visible as a backdrop to the lodge. Our "mountain" might only be a foothill compared with the Alps, but it was beautiful—and British.

"What a charming chalet," I remarked to no one in particular.

"Yes, isn't it?" my colleague agreed. "Let's just hope that what we find inside is half as charming. He addressed the Inspector. "Twigg, I thought you said the locals would be here. I don't see any police vehicles in the parking lot."

The Scotland Yarder glanced that way with displeasure.

"Perhaps the road is out. Last night's storm seems to have been a good deal worse at this elevation."

"And tonight's probably will be as well," I reminded them. "We had better conduct our business and bid a hasty farewell."

We stomped our feet clean on the porch and walked into a spacious, brightly lighted lobby. Several guests—probably skiers—were lounging around playing checkers, watching television, or just talking. The night clerk behind the desk seemed pleased at seeing a new face.

"Good evening, gentlemen. May I interest you in some rooms?"

"You already have," Geoffrey assured him. "We'd like Hugh Evans'."

Twigg flashed his badge, and the squirrelly looking clerk swallowed his smile.

"Yes, indeed! Now let me see . . . Where is he staying. Oh, yes . . . in 212. That's in the building to your right as you leave." He pulled a key out of one of the pigeon holes behind him and presented it to the Inspector. "I don't want any difficulties, officers." He lowered his voice to a stage whisper. "Would you please keep your visit as quiet as possible. We wouldn't want to hurt business, now would we?"

"We'll try to be inobtrusive," Twigg whispered just as loudly. "I hope landing a police helicopter on the front lawn didn't give us away."

We started to walk off, but Geoff had second

thoughts and turned to confront the employee again.

"Do your records show that Mr. Evans made or received any long distance telephone calls this afternoon?"

"I don't have to consult any records," the night man answered suavely. "The telephones have been inoperative all day."

Weston thanked the man for his trouble, and we strolled back into the cold. After a brief search we stood at the door to number 212. I gave it a sharp rap with the knocker and we waited.

The door opened to the end of the chain and a smallish man peered out at us through the crack. He had swarthy skin and—even wearing a bathrobe—appeared lithe and well-muscled. Twigg, a burly policeman to the last, took the direct approach.

"Are you Hugh Evans?"

"Yes. But what business is it of—"

"Inspector Twigg of Scotland Yard. We have some questions to ask you."

"All right, governor. If you'll wait a minute so I can get decent."

Hugh seemed apprehensive—to say the least—as he closed the door. A night visit by the Yard was not something to be taken lightly. We hardly had time to become impatient, though, before we heard fumbling with the chain and were invited in. As we walked past Evans, the reason for his visit to the chalet became obvious. The floor at the foot of his bed was piled high with mountain-climbing equipment.

"I see you're going to scale a rock face or two," Geoffrey observed.

The man now seemed more self-assured. His voice was firm.

"Yes. I was planning to get to sleep early in order to catch the first light tomorrow. But I'm not aware that that's illegal."

Twigg eyed him sharply.

"Who do you know that is an acquaintance of both Bertram Seawell and James Chester?"

"Why, no one." Evans seemed surprised by the question. "Some of the laboratory technicians might have been on casual terms, but nothing 'first name.' "

"Do you know of anyone," I asked, "who has a motive for killing you?"

"For what? What kind of foolishness is this?"

"Simply answer the question," the Inspector directed.

"Of course not! I'm not some back-alley billy. Let me see your identification."

Twigg handed him his wallet and the man studied both the badge and the written credentials as though looking for a counterfeit. Then he reluctantly returned the material.

"You would appear to be legitimate. But I still don't understand why you've come."

"We're here," Geoffrey declared levelly, "because someone has murdered Chester and attempted to murder Seawell. And Bertram thinks you may be the next in line."

Hugh deflated onto the edge of the bed.

"That's horrible . . . incredible!" He really appeared shaken. "Is Mr. Seawell all right?"

"No," Twigg confided, "he is not. And it's our job to keep anything from happening to you."

Weston stared thoughtfully at the equipment and then addressed Evans.

"I assume you're not foolish enough to climb alone. Are your team members staying here at Brookshire?"

"Yes. They're sleeping next door."

"Then might I suggest that you and Twigg toddle over there for a chat while John and I inspect your gear."

"If you wish," Hugh responded lamely. "But everything is in order. I've already tested the line."

"I'm sure you have. By the way, what position do you take on the team?"

"Lead climber."

"Very enterprising of you," Geoffrey complimented. "Now if you'll just *lead* Inspector Twigg next door, my partner and I will make our investigation."

Twigg was more than eager to comply. I think he suspected that there might be a hired assassin in the group. And if there were, Filbert was the man to catch him. The two ambled outdoors leaving us alone. My partner surveyed the pile with great attention to detail.

"John, I doubt whether the rope has been cut on the inside—although that's possible. Up until now our foe has shown intimate knowledge of his victims, and if he has tampered with anything, it will probably be with something vital to the top climber. Fortunately this madman has not attempted wholesale murder. Check the bongs and flukes for poison. But don't touch them. We may be dealing with a compound absorbed through the skin."

I looked in bewilderment at the mass of chain links, distorted nails and 'window scrapers.'

"What, pray tell, is a 'bong'? It sounds like a grandfather clock ringing the hour."

"They're over there," Geoffrey gestured helpfully, "by the crampons and carabiners."

"I'm delighted that you have explained yourself so clearly," I enthused tongue-in-cheek. "Now if you'll be good enough to define those latter terms."

Geoffrey nudged some metal plates off the heap with his shoe.

"These, John, are bongs and flukes. Mountaineers wedge them into crevices."

"And all the while," I grinned, "I thought those were greeting cards made of petrified Swiss cheese."

Weston and I both took out our magnifiers now and went to our hands and knees. With my nose close to the ground I looked at the strange squares from every angle. The aluminum surface appeared to be completely clean. Meanwhile Geoff was following the same procedure with some small nails and spiked shoe bottoms. At length I sat up and stretched.

"Perhaps," I suggested, "we should be back in Faversham looking for death traps in Evans' house. There doesn't appear to be anything here."

Geoffrey didn't even glance up from his task.

"We can do that at our leisure. But right now I

want to be sure the man survives to go home. Everything does seem safe to touch. I think I'll have a look at the rope—even if it is an unlikely target. You check the remainder of the hardware for explosives. The ice axe and some of the pitons—long nails—could be rigged."

Geoffrey began compressing the rope inch by inch to see if any of the interior strands might have been cut with a bladed needle. And I approached the axe with great caution—inspecting for signs that a core might have been drilled out and later plugged. I found evidence of rust but not of tampering. The pitons told the same story. Some of the smaller ones were folded over like fortune cookies and had dirt wedged in the crack, but there was no explosive device—although there might have just barely been room for one. Then I came across some hollow aluminum tubes with screw threads near one end and a ring at the other. I could make out writing on the ring.

"What," I asked, "is a 'Salewa'? It looks like a foot-long hollow sword—complete with finger guard."

Weston looked up and shook his head at my ignorance.

"A Salewa, John, is an ice piton. One hammers it in a few inches, sticks the end of the ice axe in that 'finger guard' and twists the spike farther into the ground. Then the last man up pulls it out."

"Well," I commented, "they might have gotten it out of the ground, but they certainly didn't get the ground out of it. Every one of these is plugged up."

Geoffrey frowned and came over.

"Let me have a look at that." He peered appraisingly into both ends of one of the tubes. "It seems natural enough, but . . . Get a coat hanger from the closet."

I obliged and then unbent the wire for him. Geoffrey broke off a piece and began using it to clean out the first piton. With the light touch of a watchmaker, he scraped it around the quarter-inch-wide cavity—shaving off one layer of dust at a time. I snapped off another section of coat hanger and began following the same procedure on another piton. It was painstaking work. Three Salewas and three-quarters of an hour later I felt like a fool. But then I heard Geoffrey's grim whisper.

"Here it is." He held one of the tubes at an angle so I could see the metalic glint inside. "That's a primer embedded in plastic explosive. The first tap with a hammer would have blown Evans right off the face of the mountain."

I shuddered. We were up against some sort of a fiend!

"Well," I breathed, "that would seem to remove Hugh as a suspect. It's a pity we have several dozen left."

Geoffrey stared at the piton for a long moment.

"No, John, the field is much more limited than that. In fact, I think I know who the murderer is. The problem is going to be proving it." He got to his feet and gathered together the Salewas. "We'll take these home with us for minor alterations. Tomorrow we may have a use for them."

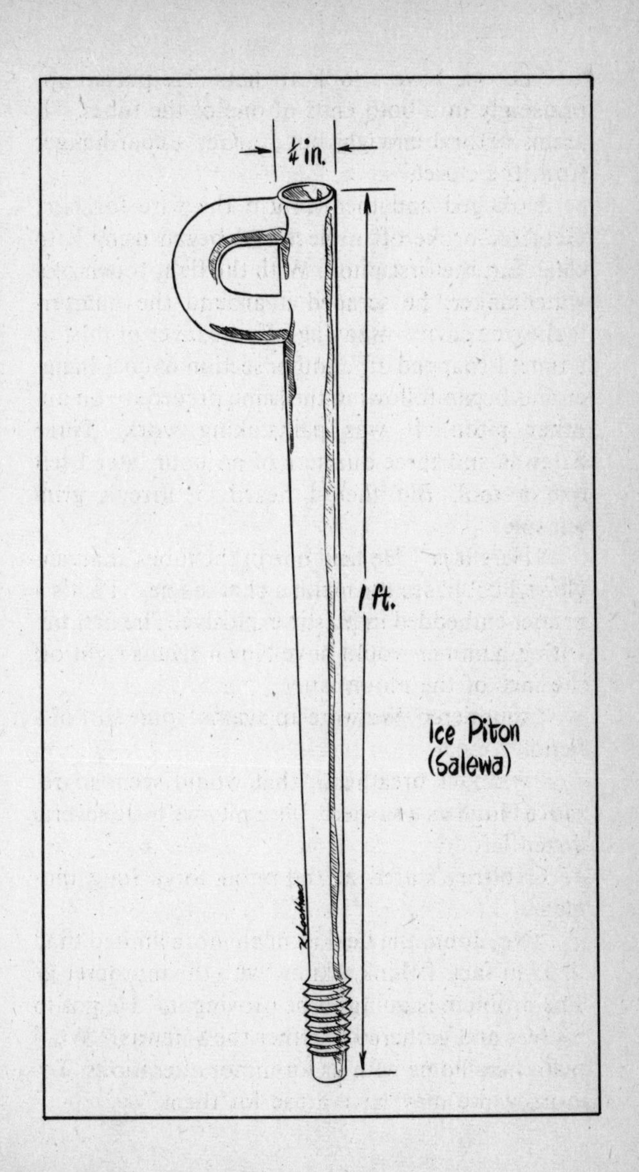

¼ in.
1 ft.
Ice Piton
(Salewa)

The Inspector, my partner and I had a wild ride back to London. Our helicopter was just ahead of the approaching storm and bobbed like a cork in the turbulence. Geoff and I found the experience invigorating. But I noticed that Filbert was a little green around the edges as he sat there with the bomb in his lap. He did not seem to appreciate, either, the clanking of the remainder of the pitons in our bag.

In spite of the distractions it was possible to lay out our strategy for tomorrow. Geoff presented Twigg with a list of suspects, and (after some prodding) the Scotland Yarder agreed to supply transportation. In a few hours about a dozen of us were going to return to Brookshire Lodge for a class in "suspect mountaineering." If all went well, we might "come up" with the murderer.

As our craft approached the police heliport, Twigg used the wireless to arrange for ground transportation. We no sooner touched down when two motorcars sped to the edge of the pad and opened doors wide to receive us. The Inspector took one back to the Yard. Geoffrey and I stepped into the other and were subjected to the swiftest tour of London that I think I've ever had. Constable Porter had been instructed to get us home "as quickly as possible," and he was evidently given to literally interpreting orders.

We came to a halt on Baker Street just as snowflakes began falling. The windows of our house were frosted over, and icicles hung like stalactites from the fence. It was a beautiful sight, and I was glad to be back. Our chauffeur waved a perfunctory farewell and left us standing at the curb.

"I think," Geoffrey commented wryly as we watched the man skid onto Marylebone, "that the Inspector has had his revenge on us for presenting him with that bomb. Let's go settle our stomachs with some hot chocolate."

I worked the key into the gate with some difficulty and twisted. Nothing happened.

"You're going to have to heat up the lock a bit first," I observed. "It's iced over."

Weston took out his pocket knife and began chipping away the glaze. Another try turned the key ever so slightly.

"We've almost got it," my colleague assured me. "A little more working back and forth and . . . What's that?" He bent down to examine the space between the gate and gate post. His next words were so soft I could hardly make them out. "John, let's get down on our knees and thank the Lord for ice. If we had opened that gate, it would have been the last thing we ever did."

Geoffrey inserted his pen knife in the crack and worked loose the end of a strip of what looked like modeling clay. He was very careful not to disturb the detonator until the explosive was removed. Then we kneeled in the snow and gave thanks. We prayed also for the poor devil who had attempted to take our lives.

When we tried the lock again it worked loose with a minimum of effort, and we walked the few steps to the house. Geoff retreated to the kitchen to heat up the chocolate while I piled logs on the hearth and stirred up the embers. I could hear him in the other room accompanying his efforts with an off-key version of "A Mighty Fortress Is Our God." And it sounded VERY good. When the fire caught, I picked up Gladstone and walked into the kitchen whistling that same hymn.

Muffins were browning in the toaster and milk for hot chocolate was simmering on the stove. I rinsed out a couple of cups and sat down.

"Why," I asked, "do you suppose the killer booby-trapped the gate?"

Weston shoveled some cocoa into the pot and stirred.

"I presume because he knows we're a threat to him. And he could hardly have reached the house with his device without leaving footprints in the snow. Don't worry, old chap. There weren't any. I looked. And no one has been around back either."

"What do you propose we do to protect ourselves?"

"Aside from calling the Yard," Geoffrey declared solemnly, "there's not much we can do—except perhaps keep Gladstone inside."

"Keep the cat in!"

"Certainly. The murderer might dip its claws in cyanide and train it to attack us."

I couldn't tell whether Weston was serious or not, but decided to maintain our pet's indoor status. Geoffrey poured the hot chocolate and started to sit down when the doorbell rang.

"I'll get it, John. Be a good fellow and jelly the muffins when they pop up."

I did just that and still had my knife poised when Weston returned carrying a large official-looking envelope. Twigg was a man of his word!

My partner spread the contents across the table, sat down, and held his cup in one hand while he leafed through papers with the other.

"Now this," he remarked," is most gratifying. Along with the information about the witnesses, the Inspector has included some preliminary material on the college staff—including class schedules. There's almost nothing on Consolidated's workers, though." He stopped for a bite of muffin. "Most of what Twigg says about the patients and witnesses duplicates what we already know. But a couple of added details may prove helpful. While you're out gardening, I think I'll make some telephone calls."

I choked on my chocolate and doubled over trying to clear my throat.

"What," I finally managed, "are you talking about? I assure you I have no plans of planting daffodils in the snow."

My partner chuckled.

"You'll be planting Salewas, John, not daffodils. After you clean out the rest of the tubes to check for surprises, I want you to go out back and clog them up again with dirt. A few moments drying in the oven should make them indistinguishable from what you started with."

"Then you're going to use the pitons as bait."

Geoffrey nodded.

"Not exactly as bait, but that's close enough. I would appreciate it if you'd postpone asking any further questions until tomorrow. I want to get this reading done in time to call people while they're still awake."

The request seemed reasonable so I ate on in silence. Geoffrey became totally absorbed in analyzing the reports.

After finishing my snack, I gathered in the pitons from the living room and soaked them in the bathtub to soften their contents. The procedure proved so effective that I was able to finish scraping out the rest of the lot within an hour. There were no other bombs. It took an additional fifteen minutes to locate the right kind of soil and to stuff the tubes to the correct levels. When I returned to the kitchen to bake my masterpiece, Geoffrey was just concluding his last telephone call. He came walking in with a broad smile on his face.

"You look," I observed, "like the cat who ate the canary. What have you found out?"

Weston tried his best to appear nonchalant but never quite succeeded. The excitement in his voice betrayed him.

"There's a bit of good news, old boy. For one thing the Yard has agreed to watch our house for us. And I've managed to learn a thing or two about the murderer."

"That's it?"

"Well, there was one other thing. A young lady called and told me to give you a message. It seems Twigg has been spreading around our telephone number again."

"Weston," I complained, "sometimes talking to you is like pulling teeth. What did she say?"

Geoffrey smiled so hard it must have hurt.

"She said she liked the books . . . and that she became a Christian at nine-thirty this evening."

CHAPTER 8

To Sleep, Perchance to Scream

Mt. Snowden glistened in the afternoon sun—reflecting a rainbow of colors from the ice and snow. One of its jutting granite cliffs now loomed above us and blocked out the eastern sky. Weston, Twigg and I were awaiting the arrival of our suspects. The preparations had been made. Hugh Evans had loaned us the use of his climbing gear. And we were dressed for the Arctic. The Inspector, however, was less than happy. His words oozed gloom.

"This had better work, Weston, or you and I are both in trouble. I can just see myself in the accounting department, trying to justify a winter vacation for thirteen on lovely Mt. Snowden!"

Geoffrey looked steadily at the four-wheel-drive vehicles coming up to meet us. The gleam of the chase was in his eye.

"If we fail, my friend, I will personally pay those expenses. But I do not anticipate failure. Be alert. There may be violence."

Pines and hickories dotted the countryside in front of us. A majestic mountain was at our backs. It seemed an unlikely spot for the sinister, but I sensed that my partner was correct. I viewed the approach of our guests with considerable uneasiness.

The jeep station wagons churned up the last slope and came to a halt slightly to our right. Two uniformed policemen stepped out followed by an unusual assortment of pseudo-mountain climbers. June Albey was the only one who really seemed happy about being there. I could see by her eager chatter that she considered it an adventure. Ruth Chester had a proud bearing and purposeful stride as she walked toward us. Sandra Meyer was dressed stylishly for the occasion and walked arm in arm with Stephen Hill. Singleton and Davidson, the two negative personalities in the crowd, were enjoying complaining to one another about the shabby treatment they were receiving. Jackson Smyth and Hugh Evans followed slightly behind the others.

As they all gathered around, Inspector Twigg addressed the group with the air of someone used to taking charge. His chunky strength was reassuring.

"Good afternoon, ladies and gentlemen. I want you to know that I deeply regret the inconvenience that this meeting has caused for some of you. But I want to stress the gravity of the situation as the Yard sees it. One man has been killed and another is in critical condition. An attempt was made on Mr. Weston's and Mr. Taylor's lives last night. And we have reason to believe that one or more of you may also be in danger.

"We are here today at the request of Geoffrey

Weston. As you are already no doubt aware, his methods are unorthodox. But the man has shown phenomenal success in solving certain types of crimes, and I expect your complete cooperation. Geoff, the show is all yours."

My partner stepped forward and looked from face to face. There wasn't a cough or a whisper. Everyone's attention was riveted on him.

"Thank you, Inspector." His manner was firm and reasonable. "You are probably all wondering right now why we're standing here in front of a pile of climbing equipment. I assure you that the answer will be forthcoming in a few moments. So please be patient. For now I will say only that we owe Mr. Evans a debt of gratitude for loaning the gear to us." He nodded appreciatively in Hugh's direction.

"Everyone here is a suspect. And one of you is a killer. I know that for a fact. I even know who it is. And I give the assassin warning right now. You will be dealt with in a manner befitting your crime. A surprise has been prepared that will end your deadly career!"

Geoff paused and gazed coolly at the assembly. I noticed Jackson Smyth and Sandra Meyer drop their eyes.

"Now," my partner picked up the thread of thought, "let's examine each one of you in the light of the evidence. Mrs. Chester, you had the opportunity to murder your husband. He could have reached home and then been disposed of by you."

Our client flushed in anger.

"Mr. Weston, this is outrageous! I *hired* you to find the killer."

"Yes," Geoffrey considered, "you did. But that could have been a ploy to divert suspicion from yourself. Your husband was not as ethical as you told us. And you did not rate yourself as very exciting to him. If (and this is only conjecture) he had an affair with, say, Mrs. Seawell, you would then have a motive for both killing him and for sending a deadly package to Faversham. You had access to your husband's office and laboratory and had an elementary knowledge of behavioral psychology which could have enabled you to train the chimp."

Mrs. Chester's brown eyes flashed in defiance. "I don't even know Mr. Seawell! And I assure you I loved my husband. You're a horrid man!"

"Love rejected," Geoffrey continued in a reflective mood, "is a leading cause for murder. But there's a fatal flaw in my theory. You knew that your husband had a chrome hip joint. If you were guilty, you never would have tried to hide the crime by cremating him. What's more, I doubt that you have enough strength to have dragged a corpse over a six-foot stone wall into the cemetery. No, Mrs. Chester, you are innocent."

Geoffrey stooped over a pile of Salewas and selected one. He then handed it, along with an ice axe, to Ruth.

"It's now time for your lesson in mountaineering. Please take this piton over to that wall, hammer it into the ice, and leave the axe there for the next person." He pointed to a spot about ten feet away.

"Do I have to?" The woman seemed confused.

"Humor me," Geoffrey commanded firmly.

Obviously relieved yet showing signs of the struggle within her, she walked over to the cliff and vented her frustrations on its granite face.

Geoffrey now turned to the next suspect.

"Mr. Evans, you knew both Bertram and James. You worked with the monkeys. And you had opportunity to form antagonisms. But I doubt that you're the murderer."

Hugh visibly relaxed.

"It's good to hear you say so, Mr. Weston. And I would like to state for the record that I liked both men."

"I'm sure you did," Geoffrey agreed. "And the fact that the telephone lines here were down at the time of the attack on Seawell is evidence of your innocence (barring the existence of some accomplice). Here's a Salewa. Give it a couple of raps."

Hugh took the piton from Weston and pounded it into the cliff ice, completing the operation with a few twists of the screw.

My partner now surveyed the group with a perplexed frown.

"It would seem, ladies and gentlemen, that we are coming to an impasse. You, Professor Davidson, might have felt some professional jealousy toward Chester, but that is hardly a motive for murder. And I am unable to uncover any connection between you and Seawell at all. What's more you teach a class from ten to ten-fifty Tuesday mornings. The stolen holographic projector had no remote control capability, so you are almost surely not the man who turned it on. Someone would have seen the image long before ten forty-two if you had flipped a switch before the lecture. And, even if they hadn't, the machine would have run out of film before the last sighting at eleven. That removes you from suspicion. Here's your piton."

Professor Davidson was so happy to escape the suspect category that he was almost cheerful as he flailed away at the spike. His hammer blows were both energetic and accurate.

"That leaves us," Weston continued levelly, "with five possible assassins." He paused to blow on his hands. "Every one of you is a student. And all but one of you were patients of James Chester. You patients had a motive for killing the man. It's not pleasant to undergo the kinds of treatment that he evidently dished out. But if one of you had murdered the professor for that reason, why would you have attacked Seawell? You would have had no cause. I conclude, therefore, that we do not as yet know the true motive for the violence we've seen."

Geoffrey ignored the pile of pitons and picked the next Salewa from a back pack lying in the snow. He handed it to Stephen Hill.

"It's your turn now, young man. Give it all you've got."

The balding athlete looked searchingly at Weston.

"I'll knock it right through the mountain, but I certainly don't understand what you're trying to prove."

He walked over to the cliff wall, picked up the

axe, and positioned the piton on the ice. His arm went back . . . and he hesitated—struggling against indecision.

"The game's up, Stephen." Geoffrey's voice was soft—almost soothing. "You made too many mistakes."

Hill now turned to face us and forced a salesman's smile to his mouth.

"Why, what do you mean, Mr. Weston? I've simply realized how silly this game of yours is, and I've decided not to play."

"Hammer the piton in," my partner demanded coldly, "or stand condemned for Chester's murder."

Stephen's smile faltered, then vanished altogether.

"I will not. And you can't prove a thing against me. You're going to pay for this slander."

"I doubt that," Geoffrey responded. "You won't hit the Salewa because you're afraid to. You tried to kill me last night. Perhaps I'm returning the favor today. You can't quite convince yourself that the tube in your hand isn't the one you booby-trapped."

"Booby-trapped?" Hill raised his eyebrows. "Surely you're not talking about a bomb!"

Weston scowled.

"All the acting talent in the world won't change the facts, young man. I should have been suspicious right from the start when you 'thought' you smelled Chester's cigar. But you were devilishly clever about the way you made your statement—trying to throw us off the track but injecting just enough doubt to save your skin in the event we discovered the truth. Then there was the matter of the time at which you saw Chester's image. The murderer had obviously turned on the projector for the benefit of students changing classes. But you made your sighting eight minutes early. Why? Because you were the one who set up the machine!"

"That's a lie!" Stephen looked about uneasily, seeking support but not finding any. "I had no reason to—"

"Oh, yes, you did," Geoff cut him off. "*Only* you had a motive for all the attacks. And you invariably left your trademark. James, the man who trained monkeys for FREEZING, was BURNED. Bertram, the man who FREEZES, was attacked by a monkey that had been FROZEN. And Hugh, who also worked in cyrogenics, was to be blown apart by an ICE piton.

"Mr. Hill, a slice of your life is unaccounted for—including, not surprisingly, the year James Chester was fitted with his joint. That's why you didn't know about it. And those many months were not spent wandering the world as a hippy. I called your family doctor last night. He says that six years ago you were terminally ill. How long were you frozen, waiting for a cure? Three years? Four? But the doctors didn't take into account that eternal consciousness deep inside of you, did they? They didn't believe you had a soul. And you were like the man in the Francis Bacon painting I saw once at the Hayward Galleries. You were trapped in a transparent cube—a block of ice—

screaming one long, frozen scream. How hideous a thought! Four years shrieking in mute torment . . . hemmed in by cold bones . . . unable to flee to heaven or even be cast into hell! No wonder it drove you mad. And no wonder you were bent on murdering the men who experimented on you."

While Geoffrey was speaking, Hill's expression changed. His jaw muscles hardened and his eyes narrowed into slits. All of the humanity seemed to drain out of him, being replaced with the look of the hunted, mixed with cold rage. His axe hand raised—holding us at bay.

"You're a clever devil!" he shouted. "But you can never know what it was like—to be so utterly alone. Stuck on the shelf like some worthless machine! Yes, I killed Chester. He deserved it. He was the toad that talked me into the thing in the first place. And then he had the gall to 'treat' me afterwards with his electric shocks and juvenile rewards. Giving me candy as though I were one of his monkeys!" Hill tossed away the piton and grabbed a knife from his belt with the left hand. "I killed him. And after you're dead, I'll go after that heartless worm, Evans. Which do you want—a dagger or an axe in your chest?"

Weston motioned his companions to back away.

"I am aware, Stephen, that you're an accomplished knife-thrower and can no doubt carry out that threat. And I'm not going to say the thought doesn't bother me. You wouldn't believe that." Geoff glanced at Twigg and the bobbies who were working their way to both sides of the man. "Even

Jesus sweated drops of blood while thinking of the pain involved in dying. But if I die it won't be to spend an eternity screaming. I'm going to a warm, pleasant heaven where I can pass my days talking and laughing with people who love me."

"That's a rotten *lie*!" Stephen Hill crouched with his back to the granite wall like some cornered beast. "I've been there! Death is a frozen hell!" He looked wildly to his sides. "Don't get another step closer or I'll throw. I mean it!"

Twigg and his men hesitated and then pulled back. My partner wiped beads of perspiration from his brow. But that was the only sign of stress that I could see. His voice remained even.

"Mr. Hill, if you throw that axe, I walk through a doorway into beauty. But you walk into a tiny, cold prison cell with bars of steel. There you'll spend twenty, thirty, forty years waiting to die. And after death, what then?

"You're afraid of closed spaces. That's the real reason the alarm in the crematorium went off, isn't it? You were so unnerved by that tiny space and those clogged windows that you went running outside in a panic and broke the wires. If only a few moments does that to you, think of what a lifetime will be like!"

Tears were now flowing down Stephen's contorted cheeks. He was almost pleading.

"But I've got to kill them, don't you see? They have to be punished. They have to suffer."

"The men at Consolidated," Weston assured him, "will be punished for any and every law they've broken. But vengeance doesn't belong to you. Give up the vendetta. There's a place where you can stay that has no bars. And I'll come to visit you, I promise. We can talk about someone who really died and who came back from the grave."

The young man began sobbing uncontrollably. His grip on the axe and dagger loosened. They dangled for a moment—then fell into the snow. Stephen doubled over, weeping the tears that had remained frozen inside of him for half a decade.

Twigg and the bobbies now closed in and kicked away the weapons. Stephen Hill was grabbed by strong arms and had handcuffs slapped onto his wrists. He was searched and then led away. We all stood stunned at the sudden turn of events. The case of the frozen scream was closed.

Epilogue

Later that afternoon Geoffrey, Twigg, Miss Albey and I sat around the kitchen table at 31 Baker Street and discussed the case over tea and biscuits.

"I still don't understand," I admitted, "why Seawell and Evans didn't tell us about Stephen Hill from the first. They must have known he was after them."

"Of course they did," Weston agreed. "But think a moment about the definition of death. A man is now considered dead when he has a flat brain wave. And people with flat waves can't be put into suspended animation and revived. Stephen Hill was literally frozen alive! And he was probably not the first. How many before him, I wonder, died during the thawing process? And each of those deaths would probably be ruled murder by the courts. Bertram couldn't as much as admit Hill's existence without ruining Consolidated Cryogenics and subjecting its staff to prosecution."

June looked pensively into her teacup.

"But if that's the case, all Steve had to do for revenge was to blow the whistle on what was happening."

"He couldn't do that," Twigg disagreed, "without branding himself as a freak as well as a possible lunatic. Self-image can be extremely important to a person. What I don't understand is why Hill didn't lie about the length of the cigar—adding an inch or two. That certainly would have strengthened the illusion that Chester was alive."

"Even I can answer that one," I declared. "Stephen probably didn't know the burning rate, so he wouldn't have known how much to add. He also couldn't know when the next witness had seen the projection. It would have aroused suspicions—to say the least—if the cigar lost two inches in as many minutes. And he must have also guessed we would check the amount of ash as well as the victim's buying habits. On at least that one point he had to stick with the truth—at least the truth of the illusion."

My colleague munched thoughtfully on a biscuit.

"Isn't it ironic? The man was driven insane by humanists who never quite fathomed what they'd done. And now he will be committed to an institution controlled by individuals of the same bankrupt philosophy. I'm going to be praying for the rest of Chester's patients and for Seawell, to be sure. But I feel the most burdened about Stephen Hill. The man was as much a victim as he was a murderer.

"I expect I'll be visiting him next week. If any of you would like to come along, you're welcome. Stephen needs friends. And he needs to hear about the love and forgiveness that Christ still offers him. I'd appreciate it, Twigg, if you could pull a few strings to get me through the doors. And there's one other thing. I know of a Christian psychiatrist who might be willing to donate his time for work with the lad. Would it be possible to obtain permission for that?"

"I'll do what I can," the Inspector promised. He shook his head in amazement. "After seeing your bravery in the face of death today, I'm beginning to think there's something to your evangelical brand of Christianity."

I put down my cup and looked soberly across the table at Twigg.

"There is," I replied. "Let me tell you about it."